SURVIVED
and
THRIVED

THE LAST TABOO

Mike Bruckner

PAGE PUBLISHING, INC.
New York, NY

First originally published by Page Publishing, Inc. 2017

ISBN 978-1-68409-816-3 (Paperback)
ISBN 978-1-68409-818-7 (Hard Cover)
ISBN 978-1-68409-817-0 (Digital)

Printed in the United States of America

FOREWORD

I am humbled by the fact that everyone mentioned in this book has given me permission to use their real names. This is such a taboo subject, and to have such support from my loved ones for this project is astounding. Even those who don't share my final thoughts on my mother, even those who appear as not perfect, all of them did not hesitate to allow me to use their names. So when you read a name here, it means something a little more than just seeing the real names in print. What it means to me is a bevy of brave souls who value honesty, who are brave enough to let me speak the truth as I see it and who love me enough to support me one more time in my journey of healing.

For all you brave readers, here is some advice from a man who is not perfect, a man who has had to overcome tremendous pain and abuse and still came out the other side with people who love me and whom I adore. If you have feelings of anger, if you feel unsettled, if you feel despair and can't seem to go on, fake it till you make it. It took me years, it was hard work—no, exhausting work. But if you take those first steps and then just feel your way along, trusting in your mentors and others who have been there before you, you CAN get through anything. You will notice all those feelings listed above start to fade away—slowly at first—then faster. Until you can finally say, "I get it!"

—Mike Bruckner

This book is dedicated to my spouse and best friend, Robin.
Although Robin was not physically or sexually abused,
she has been by my side for thirty-four years and has witnessed
the dark underbelly of this sad epidemic. Robin has suffered
as a result of my dysfunction. My prayer is for us to continue
to move beyond the pain and enjoy our life together.

A special "thank you" to my therapist, crisis counselor, life coach, referee and friend, Dr. Brenda B. Bary, PhD.

Yes, I do believe in angels.

Special Note to the Victims of Jerry Sandusky:

I am from the Philadelphia area and an avid football fan. When the news of Jerry Sandusky broke, it was a shock to my system. I was glad it went national, and that people were taking the story very seriously. In the weeks ensuing after his arrest, a torrent of admissions emerged following that first allegation. They have evoked deep emotion in me and have opened some secret compartments still buried in my head. I had been thinking of writing this book for many years, now I know I can't hold off. The world needs to hear these things.

I am sorry for what has happened to you. Most people are sorry for what has happened to you. You probably will ask yourself the proverbial question: "why me?" My answer to you is simple: why not? We live in an imperfect world with imperfect people. Most of these people are good, but not all. Your life was impacted by one of these bad people.

So now what? Get help, talk to a therapist. If the therapist is not helping, find another that will. Heal and thrive! I know, I have been there.

Your lives have been altered forever. *If* and *where* you end up will be up to you. Unfortunately, not everyone makes it, as the work is difficult.

My prayer for you is the courage, self-love and determination it takes to see it through.

Now you are called a survivor of child sexual abuse. Learn how to be a "thriver." Always remember, *you* make the ultimate decision.

I wish you a healthy, happy life filled with love and trust; it's possible…there is hope!

CHAPTER 1

A Perfect Summer Day

A family in harmony will prosper
in everything.

—Chinese proverb

Even if you don't have grandchildren, I think you can relate to how perfect this scene is. I am sitting on my couch with one grandson (eighteen months) on my knee and a granddaughter (two years old) crawling up my leg. They are both laughing and looking right into my eyes.

"Poppy," she gurgles and holds her arms out to me.

The light is catching on her blonde hair, hair that is still very thin, still more like a baby's hair than a little girl's. A man couldn't feel any happier, any more content than I feel right now. This is life in all its perfection. I pull her up onto my other knee and lean toward the top of her head. I breathe in a light scent of *No More Tears* shampoo and smile. I think to myself that I used that shampoo when I was little. The innocent smell of the shampoo is just one of many thousands of little things that connect me to my family, to life.

My arms are stretched out wide and circle both of them. They face each other and jabber away. I'm sure they know what they are saying, I have no clue. What is obvious is that they are happy, carefree and have no thought of danger or pain. Just the way every child should grow up. I didn't have that type of childhood. Because I didn't, I find that no matter how hard I try to push the thought from my mind, whenever I am with my grandchildren (like I am this summer morning), I think over and over again to myself, "How can anyone hurt something so sweet and innocent as a young child?"

I am proud my own children turned out to be such wonderful parents. I am amazed that through it all, I was able to bring up three wonderful children who are well-adjusted and living normal lives. There is a lot to be said for a normal life. A life where parents love their children, and children grow up and still love their parents; sounds so simple.

My first child was a son, Chad. Chad has grown up to look a lot like me. He served in the military, which made me very proud; yet I was nervous and worried about every single hour he served out his tour of duty in Iraq. He is now a police officer, and I am still so very proud of him. Chad married a great woman by the name of Kristin. Kristin is a first-grade teacher who is a great wife and mother. We're proud to have her in our family.

My second child was a daughter, Lindsay. Most of her career she has worked as an oncology nurse (cancer patients). She recently transitioned into a part-time position whereby she can work at a local hospital and earn a full-time income while being there for her four children. She met her husband when he was an EMT at a local hospital. Scott is now a full-time police officer. He is a talented guy who is able to do all their home renovations himself. To me, his best attribute is his humility; he is a hands-on dad, and anyone can see how much he loves his kids.

My third child was another son, AJ. AJ, short for Alex John, also served his country with two tours of duty in Iraq. AJ is also a police officer in a local borough. AJ shares many personality traits with me; it is so comforting and strange to have a son who speaks, moves and thinks much like I do. AJ has been married for five years to Sarah, a totally wonderful lady, and they have two beautiful girls. Currently, Sarah is a stay-at-home mom. We look at Sarah as a daughter and enjoy her big heart and quiet character. The best thing for me, Sarah adores AJ. I love to see people in love.

I take real joy in the fact that I like all the partners my children are sharing their lives with, and that they are all settled into good careers and have forward moving, solid lives. Can a father ask for more? They even still like me and come to visit often, even more often they drop the grandkids off, like today, for us to babysit while they run their errands or have a nice date night with their spouses.

I am sometimes asked where I learned my fathering skills since I didn't have a good role model for a father. I learned some very basic fathering skills from the television western starring Chuck Connors. He played the homesteader Lucas McCain on ABC's *The Rifleman*—a black-and-white TV show that ran from 1950 to 1963. I think because it was cutting edge for its time, in that it was the first program that showed a dad raising a boy alone, it had to really delve into those things we call teachable moments now, really dig into the reasoning behind any actions Lucas took with his son. Another thing I loved about this show is that it was all about second chances, overcoming faults and being a good person. Everyone did the right thing in the end; they may have struggled, they were not perfect, but they all sucked it up and did the right thing. That was a spark of hope for me.

I didn't have that kind of life, and it took me decades to work through the devastation left in my psyche from my own early years. Well, you know, there are still things that will always be a part of the dark corner of my mind. Dark memories, pain. The behaviors I adopted to survive those times—some form of them will always be with me. But it *IS* decades later, and I am babysitting two of eight darling grandchildren. I have broken a cycle that I know goes back at least three generations, and I am sitting here reaping the rewards of the hard work that my family and I put into building this good life. I define a good life both narrowly and widely—as you will see. But right now…

"Mike, bring them to the table, munchies are almost ready."

We are waiting for our snack. My wife, Robin, is whipping up their favorite: apple cobbler.

We have them for the whole day this Saturday, as Lindsay is at a conference for her job. I bought a *Slip and Slide* yesterday, and I can't wait to set that up in the backyard. This is going to be a great way to kick off summer.

I have alluded to my childhood not being perfect; well, it was horrific. Yet what was done to me is only a very small part of my story. It is a part that should be told (*will be told*) here as complete as I can. Yet the purpose of my life and this book is to show the way out of the darkness and pain. Show the progression childhood abuse can take if not addressed and show that there *is* a light at the end of any tunnel we find ourselves in. I have come out the other side of that long, dark tunnel into the sunshine. I made it out after suffering sexual, physical and emotional abuse.

There is always hope.

Always.

CHAPTER 2

Abuse: Mother to Son

*Every TWO minutes, someone in the
U.S. is sexually assaulted. Each year, there are
about 207,754 victims of sexual assault.*

—rainn.org/statistics

I must have been about three or four when my mother first began to actively molest me. I say actively because looking back, I realize that when I first began to wear underwear, she had a fascination with my penis. She would touch, hold and talk about it often. At that age, I just assumed all moms did that, it was normal. I went from this dysfunctional behavior to the next stage when I was too young to know what was really going on. Too young to have any clue of what was going on or how to stop it; I do remember that I was very uncomfortable with the situation and would do my best to avoid my mother whenever I could.

Most people can't really recall many things from early childhood. At most, things come back to many people in feelings or still pictures, mental snapshots. I can remember most of this day clear as a bell. She called me into her bedroom one afternoon. The only other person in the house was my little sister. So I walked into my mom's bedroom, not sure what was going on, but I knew something didn't feel right. Looking back now, I must have already been developing what therapists call hypersensitivity—a way that people who have been in dangerous or traumatic situations can read microexpressions on faces or pick up on subtle tones or almost invisible cues in another's body language. It helps now to learn these things. That day, I just knew something was weird in a bad way.

There was not any type of seduction. I was ordered to come to the bed and lie down next to my mother. I suppose since I was her son, she had no need to groom me, to set up a game-type atmosphere. I was three or four, basically a little toddler, laying there beside a grown woman. Obviously, I was physically incapable of penetrating her with my penis at that young age. What she did was instruct me to put my fingers inside of her. Again, not sweet, not like a partner, it was an order. An order from a volatile and mean woman. I did what she demanded, feeling the cold air over my body. There was no top sheet on the bed, no covers. My mother always used a pastel-colored bottom sheet, and that was it. At the time I had no idea how strange it was to never have a top or covering sheet.

I can't recall how that first session of abuse ended. Then a habitual program of sexual abuse began with incidents occurring around two to three times a week. The smell of her vagina began to be associated in my mind with those bad times, the odor enough to gag me. Smell is a very strong sense for humans, closely associated with our memory and feelings. You do a lot of research when you are on a path to healing, so you will get little gems from me along the way. Here is one; our sight works through four kinds of receptor cells. Our touch recognizes heat, cold, pain and pressure. But our sense of smell— well, we have well over one thousand different types of receptor cells! Not only that, but they regenerate over our entire lifetime. So something in our brains is really attuned to smells, and I can't get into all the reasons why (I'm not a scientist), but it is wrapped up with all sorts of memories, good and bad, and comes back to us in a flash. It doesn't dance around on the tip of our tongue like a name we just can't remember. It crashes into our current thoughts, pushing all else aside as we remember that smell of Grandma's furniture oil, the attic you snooped around in, or in my case, the days of sexual trauma.

It is now over fifty years since those years of abuse, and I still cannot tolerate any vaginal odor. Robin, a piece of perfection that I get to call my wife, has worked with me in our own relationship, and we have worked out our own ways of having a fulfilling intimate life together. Ways to trick that sense of smell or get around it.

There were many times when my mother had me on the bed with her and demanded I try to penetrate her. When I was younger and could not perform up to her expectations, she would put her finger in my anus. That was the most horrible feeling in the world, something going inside me like that. My whole body still tenses up when I allow that memory to come to the forefront.

How is it I do not hate all women?

It is a part of my makeup, my very being, that I am a people person. I see the good in people and am fascinated with learning about other people and how they live their own lives. I still wonder how this part of me wasn't destroyed during the times when I was being beaten or forced to stand in scalding hot water.

You see, while I was being sexually abused, my mother was not letting up on the physical or emotional abuse that I, my sister and my brothers were suffering. In a complete betrayal of trust, my mother once asked me to show her how long I could hold my breath underwater. Most kids would think, "Yippie, I get to show off." I guess I did too. When I started to show her, she held my head underwater with her hand. I remember she held it so long that I was gasping and swallowing water while I struggled to raise my head to breathe.

More than once, something would set her off, and she would stand my little sister and I (we were the oldest two and close in age) in the bathtub. She would turn the hot water on full and make us stand there as the tub filled up. We were not allowed to move.

When she could see the pain on our faces, she would say, "Is it hot enough for you yet?"

What the hell could we say to that?

The first time she did that I remember my sister and I standing in the empty tub and seeing my mother closing the drain and turning the hot water on. The water was scalding our feet, and we were jumping up and down. We were screaming to be let out of the tub! She just watched with a glazed look in her eye. Our screams seem to push her further away from reality.

That night, I remember I slept the whole night with my legs out of the covers and hanging as much of my leg over the bed as I could. I was letting the air cool my legs. My little burned legs. I also drank a lot of cold water that night. My whole body felt like a furnace turned on high.

So the next time my sister, Michelle, and I were standing in a tub with the scalding hot water creeping up our legs, we just cried quietly. Just stood there with the pressure of her hands on our bare shoulders, and our little legs turning red with first and second-degree burns. What I think we feared was that if we crossed her at this point, she might just push us under the hot water and watch us drown. Better to suffer in silence than show any defiance and face the unknown. The unknown was most likely much worse.

Many days just passed along. It was like being in a cold war with your own mother. I was quiet and tried to always be somewhere she was not. She would be sarcastic and gruff in everything that went on. Those were the good days.

I was pinched nearly every day as my mother emphasized whatever point she was trying to make. There were often times when I was hit with the buckle end of belts, which left welts on my body. I was punched, kicked and beaten with hard objects weekly; these were times when she was slipping into a rage. Once my mother tried to pull my hair off—thank God for a strong scalp! That kind of blind rage only got worse over time. It didn't take long for my siblings to learn to just shut up and take whatever was being dished out. They were oftentimes that all four of us were hit (not spanked in a normal way on the bottom) with the buckle end of a belt—hit so hard we had welts on our bodies. She would strike out wildly when in those rages, our bottoms were not the target for her weapons, our whole bodies were.

When I was around three or four, a story goes that I had supposedly reached up and "grabbed" a hot cup of coffee off the table and spilled it on myself. The burns were so bad on my young skin that I was in the hospital for a week and turned out to have second and even third-degree burns over my face, shoulder and chest. I still bear a scar from that incident on my left shoulder. I don't believe I reached for that cup of coffee! My memory is of my mother pouring that coffee on me directly and slowly, which is the only way a cup of coffee could cause so much damage. I don't know if I am projecting this next part of my memory from other events, but I swear I can see her just looking right into my eyes with no expression as she poured that coffee on me. Just watching.

Most kids who do happen to spill a cup of hot coffee on themselves get small and spread out burned areas, not massive damage like I had. If she would hold us in the bathtub and watch as our feet and legs turned red and burned, why not a cup of coffee?

One particular beating really stands out in my memory. I must have been around ten or eleven. One of my mother's favorite weapons in a beating would be for her to use the tip of one of her high-heeled shoes. When I say tip, I don't mean the top section but the bottom sharp part of a high-heeled shoe. I guess she thought a focused point of impact would inflict maximum pain. It did. After this particular high-heeled beating, my mother left my room. I looked down. She must have hit a large vein on the right side of my knee. Remember these were done in rages—she would strike anywhere. Almost immediately after I was alone in my room, my knee ballooned up. It looked like half a baseball was crammed under my skin, and it straightaway turned blue, red and ugly.

When I came down to dinner that night, my father asked, "Mike, why are you limping?"

"Mom hurt my leg."

"Are you sure? Mike, pull up your pant leg, so I can take a look at your leg."

We were all sitting around the dinner table, and they all saw it—Mom, Father, sister and brothers. I do remember that my mom did seem to be shocked at the size and color—it was an angry and ugly bulge.

"Ann, you have to be careful."

That was all that was said. A battering that could have cost me my leg.

Be careful?

Outrageous that she did it. Outrageous that this was all that was said about the matter. My siblings just sat in silence. Now you must realize something, that this statement is not blamed from me toward them. I know very well staying still and quiet was our way to survive.

I mentioned my sister in the bathtub with me. We were only one year apart; I was the oldest. Michelle was a beautiful, truly lovely, young girl. She had waist-length dark brown hair that would be the envy of any woman. Michelle was a great sister, playing and laughing with me. She would try to make peace when the house blew up with anger, but being a child limited her abilities. Michelle tried so hard to be "good" for our mother, helping around the house and learning to cook. It didn't save her. To this day, I don't know if Michelle was sexually abused by our mother. Even though I am sharing my story with my family and the world, it still is a very hard subject to talk about. Not exactly casual talk over lunch in a crowded restaurant. I don't think I have come out and directly asked Michelle this question; she has shared some things with me but never flat out said she was or wasn't sexually abused. I'm not going to push. Everything in its own time.

Here are two visuals right out of a horror story that I was a direct witness to. Michelle was dragged up a full flight of stairs by her silky long hair. My stomach rolls when my mind takes me back to this. I saw huge clumps of Michelle's hair being ripped out and held in my mother's hands. This happened to a slender, sweet young girl.

While this did not take place on the same day, it would have been the ending of the stair-dragging episode in this horror movie… Michelle was standing in my parents' bedroom getting yelled at. She was just standing there taking it like we had all learned to do. Fighting back was like asking for more abuse, and none of us were stupid.

I could see that my mother was not satisfied with just yelling; I could see Mom's expression was kind of rolling. Hard to explain but almost like her cheeks and forehead were twitching and moving because she was so restless. The yelling was not getting her off like she wanted. Whatever thrill and satisfaction she got from verbally and physically abusing us was not being touched that evening. So she amped up her rage and started to hit Michelle on the face and shoulders. My innocent sister rocked with the blows, ducked and turned a little and just tried to ride the storm out. This night, it was beyond extreme. My mother began to actually foam at the mouth; her face was getting red; the hits were getting harder, and still, I could tell she was not satisfied. I was around eight or nine years old, I had been battered and sexually abused. I knew I could not help Michelle. I stood there with my fists balled up, and my whole body tensed and wanting to dive in and pummel my mother. I loved my sister and had to watch helpless.

Still, Mom's rage was building, her skin was still twitching, and I started to feel cold fear crawl up my back. Mom grabbed Michelle's head, pulled it to her mouth and bit her on the nose. As blood dripped down Michelle's face, my mother had not lost her rhythm and was still yelling at Michelle. The blood was dripping down on the bed by the time my mother lost her energy. My mind froze at the bite; I can't remember how this incident ended. I just see blood pooling on the bed and Michelle's face and nose. *Sweet Michelle, I love you still, and I wish I could have saved you back then. You didn't deserve any of that.*

These were just some highlights of the sadistic physical and emotional abuse suffered at the hands of my mother. I'm sure I don't remember all of what happened. I do know for sure that every day was scary, every day something little happened, even if it was just a hard pinch as I walked by. Due to these constant low-level attacks, I think my siblings and I have some form of PTSD. I know the fallout from not being able to save my sister had profound effects on what is called my internal dialogue the things I would say to myself in my own mind. It made me feel weak; it made me feel like I was not a good brother. That seeped into my whole way of looking at myself. I never gave up totally. I always had a tough spot at my core. But we humans are complex and along with the tough-guy parts, I was also haunted by feelings that I was just not good enough.

We were not a social family. With this rage and these secrets, how could we have been even close to a normal family? We weren't reclusive or extreme in that aspect, occasionally a family did come over, or we did go to visit. Occasionally, a neighbor lady would come over and visit with my mother. They seemed to be friends. Yet, that was the extent of our social world. I'm not sure what my parents did for fun; I know there were scattered times when we had a babysitter. My mother considered us poor and blamed my father for not being a good provider. I had no idea or feeling of being poor; we were fed, had a home, and there was nothing materially that I yearned for.

My baby brother is born, just another soul to abuse. You have to remember that this was back in the early to mid-sixties, and birth control was a new thing; also society still expected women to have large families. I also found out in my adult life that my mother had another reason to want another child. I'll talk about that and more about her soon.

Into this den of dysfunction, my mother gave birth to my youngest brother, Stuart (Stu). Upon arriving home after the birth, she flopped Stu down on the couch and told my sister and I that we were responsible for taking care of him—then she just walked off. Now we had even more opportunity to do something wrong and get yelled at or slapped or worse. Still, we loved our little brother and did our best. Marc was only two when Stu was born, so he was not saddled with this task so far and had really not begun to realize what was going on. He was a cute innocent young boy just learning to talk and walk.

If there is a new brother on the scene, you may be thinking that she must not be a single mother, where's the dad? Is he abusive too?

My father was there the whole time. In fact, he is in his eighties now, and Robin and I have him over a couple of times a month for dinner. I talk to him a few times each week on the phone. His name is Dave, and we have a very nice relationship these days. Let me explain a little about Dave Bruckner; he has a fascinating history. My father's parents were Orthodox Jews in the Austro/Hungarian Empire. The family owned a brandy, wine and vinegar factory and sold their wares by visiting neighboring towns by horse and carriage. Yet they lived in what would later be annexed by Austria. Couldn't have been placed any worse as Hitler started his insane termination of all undesirables. His father, Leo Bruckner, was interred at the infamous concentration camp, Dachau.

Of course, there must have been changes in the world along the Austrian border at that time that lead up to later events, but the nightmare can be pinpointed as starting with *Kristallnacht*, Night of Broken Glass. It was fading into the dark of night on November 9, 1938. It was a pogrom that was planned by the Nazi Party and carried out by the SS, SA and even Hitler Youth. It was not isolated—this attack took place throughout all of Germany, Austria and some areas of Czechoslovakia. As the name implies, the shattering of glass from windows in synagogues, homes and stores with Jewish owners could be heard the whole night and into the next day. Dave was nine at the time, and he has told me he remembers hearing the glass break in their home and being very scared. Two SS soldiers broke into the house and "arrested" Leo, taking him silently in the night. The three children and Sarah (my grandmother) were forcibly relocated to Vienna. They lived in a second floor apartment directly across the street from a police station. Dave remembers the haunting sounds of the Jews who had been arrested and being tortured at that police station. Sarah knew they weren't safe; it was only a matter of time before the violence was turned on the male children. She and the Jewish community hatched a plan for survival for all the Jewish children. My father and his older brother travelled via steamship to Holland and on to London, England where they lived for two years. His mother and sister had to remain in Austria in constant danger.

London itself wasn't very safe with all the air raids, blackout curtains on every window and food rationing. Again, David was only around nine at the time and lived with a sponsor family in the same neighborhood as the sponsor family for his older brother, Alex. David would cry because he missed his brother and sister, so the sponsor families let them visit.

Leo spent fourteen months in Dachau! I can't imagine a week, let alone well over a year, being starved, tortured and not knowing if your family was alive or dead. Leo had been a winemaker with skills and ties to his community. In Dachau, he was just surviving. Leo was the first family member to touch American soil, after paying money to be able to connect to an American family who would "sponsor" him and guarantee he had a job in the U.S. Then he was finally reunited with his family! There was a picture of Leo, David (my dad), Gertrude and Alex that made a local paper. It was grainy and black and white, but I have included it in the back of this book, so you can see the smiles and feel the happiness that was there.

The paper quotes Leo as saying, "…my first concern will be to become a citizen of the United States." How cool is that attitude?

That estranged, terror-filled childhood must have placed a huge psychological scar on my father and was no doubt involved in the way he never fought back when my mother raged, letting her run roughshod over him. In addition, as my grandparents were strict, Orthodox Jews and David did not choose to raise his children in the Orthodox manner, the family relationship was strained, and we had very little contact with my grandparents or others from that side of the family. This meant there was no loving support from that entire side of my family tree as my father began to suffer the rages of his new wife. Perhaps they could have been an influence on how the marriage evolved. Family is so important. What if an aunt had come over and befriended my mother and helped her adjust to being a mother? Even if there were just regular visits where my mother might have had to be concerned about leaving marks on her children. Who knows what a little kindness and love could have done.

My father is still a quiet man who cannot tolerate confrontation. My father's only concern with this book was that it not portray Ann (my mother) in a bad light. After all the verbal and physical abuse, he took and watched his children take the abuses; he is still concerned with what others might think of her.

She would sometime rage and follow my father around the house stomping and screaming in his face about how unhappy she was and how weak and useless he was. I can see her face contorting from normal into a red-splotched mask of hatred. These rages were similar to what we now associate with bad alcoholics, yet I don't recall any alcohol abuse going on by my mother. I could have blocked that out or just not been aware of what it was. Still, I have no memories of the smell of drinks on her breath or of seeing drinks in her hands. I do remember how ugly she was to me when she was consumed by rage. Her eyes would even bulge as foam flecked from her mouth. Many times she worked herself up to such a state that foam dripped down her lower lip and ran down her chin. Spit often flying at us as she yelled.

At the time of their marriage, Ann was a lovely woman. She had medium to dark blonde hair cut into a fashionable bob. Ann's face was round, and she was of average to short height. Her heritage came from Russia, and she had the typical good looks and fair skin. In their wedding photo, she is leaning back and looking up at her new husband with affection. I never remember seeing that expression on her face as a child. I guess the honeymoon didn't last long.

As a father, I still cannot fathom not protecting your children. I have made peace with my father; I love him dearly. But I just cannot understand the thought process that was working (or not working) at the time that allowed such extensive verbal, physical and sexual abuse to go on. And yes, he did know there was sexual abuse. Did he allow that to be conscious knowledge? I don't know. I do clearly remember one argument that seemed to answer the question. They were in their bedroom in a heated argument, and my mother yelled out, "You're so pitiful even your son fucks better than you do."

That can't be interpreted in an innocent way. Did he push it out of his thoughts? Did he rationalize that she was just trying to hurt him with her words? Did he think a mother having sex with her son would not be damaging to a boy? Did he let his own embarrassment override protecting me? I'll never know. My father to this day shies away from talking about those years.

I want this subject to see the light of day. I want anyone who happens onto a situation of abuse to know it is wrong, to know it can have lifelong effects on the victim and to not be embarrassed about speaking up or somehow calling attention to the behavior—so that the child has immediate help and is removed from this damaging situation. If a person doesn't feel safe intervening, then they should, at the very least, call 911 and report the incident. No embarrassment, no sugarcoating the words, this behavior is wrong and must be recognized. The courts need to be involved in the adjudication with the focus placed on breaking the cycle. You break the cycle by breaking habits and changing thought processes. It is a very slow, painful process, but it does work. I am a witness to this process and still today work hard to continue to make appropriate changes that continue to enrich my life.

Child abuse must also be adjudicated with intense inpatient/ outpatient therapy. Was there ever an abuser who was not abused? Maybe. If there is such a creature, they have to be the exception to the rule. All this pain flows from their own painful childhood, and we must break this cycle.

Yet how hard that simple action must be when my own dad did not save his precious four children. And I know he is a good person. I know he loved us kids. I know what a lovely little girl my sister was. How innocent and sweet both she and my brothers were.

Then I let it happen to my brother Marc.

I cry every time I share this. Even now, my eyes are so full of tears that all I can see are blurry images. But I have to get this out. I have begged my brother to forgive me for what I did and what I didn't do.

I must have been around twelve. I was starting puberty, and Marc was about five or six. I have forgiven the twelve-year-old boy who I was then. My brother has forgiven me—yet it is such a powerful vision I have of those few minutes. It will never leave me as long as I live.

"Mike, bring your brother in here," came a command from my mother.

Only *here* was not the kitchen or living room, she was calling to me from her bedroom. All of us kids stayed as far away from that room as we could. The others must have sensed my dread when I went in or came out of there, and to this day, as I mentioned, I have no idea if my sister was sexually abused.

I complied. We always complied with her demands. We also tried to stay out of her way as much as possible so that we would not be around to hear any demands. But this day, I did not scatter fast enough. I was there in the living room, and she knew it. I went to get Marc. So I led my little brother into her bedroom, and I looked at him. He was sitting at the foot of the bed, his legs so short that his feet were dangling. Then I turned and walked out.

It haunts me.

CHAPTER 3

Continuation of Abuse and Suppression

The estimated number of children seriously
injured by all forms of maltreatment
quadrupled between 1986 and 1993, from
141,700 to 565,000 (a 299% increase).

—*The Third National*
Incidence Study (NIS-3)

When I was about eleven or twelve, just at the beginning of puberty, the sexual abuse stopped. It all makes sense now. I've studied this for decades—read articles, taken college courses. All in an effort to understand what happened to me, but even more, how I could heal myself and learn to take true joy from life again. One thing (among many) I found that really resonated with me and looking back at how my sexual abuse stopped is the pattern that nearly all sexual abusers have a "type" of victim. When their victim ages beyond this "type," they move on to their next victim. Ann's next victim was Marc.

So I was now free from the sexual abuse, yet the physical and emotional abuse raged on. Ann's predatory behavior continued on with another victim, another life shattered. I want this to sink into your minds. Almost all predators move on to other victims. Turning your head, ignoring the situation, will not only affect those you are observing in the moment, but those who in the future will cross paths with this predator and the future children of the victims. Perhaps going as far as the grandchildren of that person you saw being abused. A true snowball effect that poisons our society.

Around the time my mother stopped molesting me, the whole family went for a vacation to Hogback Mountain in Vermont one summer. We were planning on spending the whole week in Vermont. We had rented a lovely farmhouse; the area was rural and just so beautiful. We stuffed ourselves with maple candy at the local store. It started out to be the best time in our little lives. We had room to run, birds and rabbits to chase and the quiet that is only found in truly rural areas.

While my parents were arguing nonstop in the large farmhouse; my brothers and sister were playing in the hayloft and out in the fields. We could hear them arguing but tuned it out as best as we could and really enjoyed the farm and exploring outside. Nearby were both sheep and cows that we would pick grass for and feed over the fence. We were making the best of it and hoping against hope that our parents would settle down and stop yelling. At the very least, we were hoping they would leave us alone to enjoy this farm. However, my parents just never stopped their fighting, and we packed it in early and drove home, with them arguing the whole drive back home to Pennsylvania.

I remember around this age I had a pellet gun. I would shoot it out back at cans and trees. It helped channel some of my anger—anger I didn't even know I was feeling because it had been ever present for eight or nine years. I just knew I felt better when I heard the cans pop and saw them fly backward to bounce off the ground. I guess it gave me a small feeling of power.

I would hide the gun when I was not using it, so my mother wouldn't break it in one of her rages. I was a tough kid, but I thought I might break down and cry if that gun got snapped in two in front of my eyes.

One particular night, my mother burst into my room (I shared it with my brothers).

"Mike, give me your gun. I'm going to kill your father."

"I lost it."

"Liar! Give me that damn gun right now!"

I couldn't reply. What could I say?

That night, my pellet gun was right under my mattress. I had put it there for safekeeping. Was I going to give it to her and watch her shoot my father? Was I going to talk more and enflame her rage?

No, the only thing for me to do was shut up and take whatever was going to be in store for me. If I gave the pellet gun to her now, she might turn her rage on me because I lied to her and break my gun in half. I could even picture it in my mind; her bugging eyes boring right into mine as she snapped my gun. Or she would take my gun, forgetting about me in her rage at my father and shoot my dad with my own pellet gun. My whole body was tense. I had gone right from a deep sleep to stiff as a board.

So what was in store for me? It was being strangled. She grabbed my throat with both her hands and squeezed while also shaking my head.

"Where is it?" she shrieked.

My eyes were rolling around. My brothers were pretending to be asleep, I don't blame them. There was nothing they could do, they were so little; in fact, if they had spoken up or challenged our mother in any way, I am sure that it would have fueled her rage rather than calming her down.

Then I saw my father standing in the doorway to our bedroom. Instead of rushing over to my side to pull her off me…he was shaking his head no and looking right at me—meaning, don't tell her where the gun is. And I didn't. I don't remember what caught her attention and caused her to turn and see my father. She then just let me go, stomped up to him and continued whatever argument they were having.

Fathers are supposed to protect their children. What a betrayal. At the time, I was too young to put this into context or have the words for my feelings. Yet I felt keenly that this was completely not right, that this was more than ignoring warning signs and not asking the questions that should have been asked. He was staring at his own young son being throttled and then expecting that choking, scared little boy to protect his own hide. Of course, he should have stepped up years earlier when he had to have known on some level that I was being sexually abused (he certainly knew all three of us kids were being physically abused).

When we locked eyes that night, there was something even more elemental, primitive, that he was letting slide—an outright attack on his son. I think to myself about how I would step in front of a bullet, an axe, a car, anything to protect my own kids, from the day they were born to this day as adults.

I shared with you earlier the story about the bathtub and the beating with the high-heeled shoe. There are more, but the intensity and frequency are what matters for this story. We kids were under assault daily. We had finally stopped pleading for mercy as that had no effect and could, in fact, make the situation worse. We stopped hoping and thinking and dreaming that our father would step in and save us. I am assuming my sister and brothers had this same fantasy when they still had hope that it would get better. When I was around eight years of age, I used to fantasize that my father would step in.

"Enough!" he would shout.

"Ann, this is wrong. You have to stop this, or we are leaving you."

Then we would pack some bags and leave that house forever. Only it never happened, and it was too depressing to keep that vision alive. I let it fade out. Ultimately, there was no hope. We had to survive, that was all we could concentrate on, all we had the power to control. As we got older, we could set our hearts on being old enough to leave the house as adults and start our own lives.

I am convinced this dual betrayal and abuse heavily influenced how I interacted with other people. I am also convinced that it has colored and wounded my sister and brothers and the lives they tried to build.

Michelle recently shared with me a bizarre behavior of our mother toward her. I suppose that Ann had nothing else occupying her mind at the time, so she made up this form of torture for Michelle. Ann insisted that Michelle was sick. Michelle did not feel sick and had not complained of anything at all.

"Lie down on the bed and pull your panties down."

Now Ann inserted something into my sister's rectum, telling her it was a suppository, and it would make her feel better. Whether it was a real suppository or not, this was done with sadistic intent, done harshly and without care, done only to harm and torture.

I know that seeing me and my brothers abused, just being a witness, had also scarred Michelle deeply. My dear sister had been divorced twice. She has two children and is a grandmother. Now she gets to babysit her two grandchildren on a full-time basis, and she gets to really love some young children, like she did when we were little. I feel so much sadness and anger when I think about what Michelle has had to go through; she was a loving, caring sister, and now a loving, caring grandmother. She constantly put herself last and tended to the needs of her three brothers. I remember her cooking for us and trying to help in any way she could, doing the job a parent should be doing.

She loved her brothers so much and tried to be a mother to us, yet she was also powerless, like most children, when the next round of sexual abuse started for me.

And as it happened so many times, being sexually abused led to another incident of sexual abuse and a new abuser. For those of you reading this who have not done research about sexual molestation or never had a person in your life who went through something like this, let me briefly explain what I mean.

Without getting technical, basically when a person is abused in any way, there seems to be a trend or pattern that they will fall victim to others in a similar way. So not only are they often abused multiple times by a predator; they then often are again abused multiple times by a different predator. This is thought to be for two main reasons. *One*, abusers are skilled at spotting the actions and demeanor of people who can be bullied, charmed or forced into doing what they, the predator, wants. *Two*, the victim tends to know this type of predatory person and in a strange way, this knowledge is a comfort. They are drawn to the very people that hurt them. This is in **NO WAY** to say that the victim wants the abuse or deserves it or is even partially responsible. We are talking about the misty makeup of the subconscious, which is still being studied. Right now, we only have behavior patterns and theories to go on. If people are aware of these patterns, they can work hard to break them and create the life they want. So if one knows that after an episode of sexual or physical abuse, they are more likely to connect to a different person who will do this to them again…they can be on the lookout and may avoid that next predator.

This also brings to mind the prevalence of abuse in our society. Think about it. If our statistics say that one out of every five people will be sexually abused, that feels solid and static. I say it is the tip of the iceberg. First of all, we know that sexual abuse is underreported. That's a fact. How many of you suffered a grabby uncle or neighbor that hugged too tight for too long? Sure, that is a small thing compared to what I went through, but that is abuse, and no child should have to feel that funny feeling of something being "wrong" in what is going on.

Second, take me as an example. With the one in five statistic, you may feel you have put a label on this; you have the parameters down. I am one of the five. But think about how my abuse stretched over the years. And then think about how I was abused by another person multiple times. All these individual instances of abuse pan out to me being one of the five...but how many *times* was I victimized? Thousands, even beyond my counting. And this is what happens to many of us lost children out there. The statistics are strong, but the real stories behind these numbers are sobering and sad.

This next part is also very embarrassing to share, but I have to share for anyone else out there suffering in a similar way who thinks they are all alone. You are not alone, you may be experiencing things a little differently, but it is all connected, and it is not your fault. How embarrassing is it to poop your pants as a young kid? Well, how much more shameful if you are pooping your pants at the age of nine or ten? I refer to the bathroom as my ground zero. That is where penis touching and pulling would often occur. In order to keep my penis to myself, I would put off going to the bathroom as long as I could, which often led to not making it to the bathroom on time or even purposely pooping in my pants. I learned to do laundry at a young age. In what world is choosing to mess your pants, doing the extra wiping up and sneaking in laundry chores the best choice? Sadly, it is in the world of sexual abuse.

My second brush with sexual abuse and my second abuser was during my early puberty. I was old enough not to need a babysitter, but my brothers and sisters still did, and I was young enough not be entrusted to the care of three others. My memory is still somewhat fuzzy about this event. I did suppress it during my teen and early adult years. Totally blacked out the memory. Through therapy, I have briefly brought the memory out to look at and then locked it away. It is not something I really wanted to dig deeply into. I just had to acknowledge it and then let it go again. Just as my mother abused me, I was again abused by a female.

My brothers had gone off to bed early that night; remember they were six and eight years younger than my sister and I. I was in our living room watching TV. I don't want or need to unearth the really gritty details, but in a nutshell, it was the babysitter. She had my hands tied above my head on one of those floor-to-ceiling pole lamps so popular in the seventies. She pulled my pajamas down and stared for a while. Then she made a trip to the kitchen. When she came back, she ran an ice cube all around my penis and crotch area.

This teenager then put the ice cube aside and started to tug at my penis. Like my mother, not in a gentle partnership way, but in a sadistic way. I am sure she was looking to see pain in my face. The scary and confusing part was that while I had no interest in this babysitter as a girl I would be attracted to, it did feel good, and I did get an erection. She pulled and stroked some more.

Michelle had wandered into the room sometime during this; there was no way I could cover up and stop since my hands were tied above my head. The babysitter knew she was there but didn't seem to mind or change her actions in any way, neither paying attention to my sister nor sending her away. There really was no end to the things that battered at Michelle and killed any normal childhood for her.

Then the babysitter who was not there for me took me to my room and "tucked" me into bed where she continued to pull and tug on my erect penis for maybe ten more minutes.

I never told anyone about this. How ashamed I was that I had an erection from this. Because I never told anyone, this babysitter was used a few more times and each time she did almost exactly the same thing to me, and in my mind, I "let her" do it. As a little boy, I thought that if I had an erection, then I had to have been

36

a willing participant in that action. The same went for the times in my mother's bed when I was old enough to get an erection and penetrate her. The feelings of guilt while having pleasure. They were just overwhelming.

Talk about some negative affirmations with sexual functioning!

But negative is what it is, even when there are physical feelings of pleasure, there is no emotional pleasure and no desire for it—therefore it *is* rape, no matter how the body is responding.

Many victims of sexual abuse unfortunately get pregnant as teens, become sexually promiscuous and often become addicted to masturbation. These things may seem to defy common sense. Shouldn't a victim become cold and fearful of any sex? That is what many victims think too and then heap guilt on top of guilt when they find themselves following these aberrant sexual behaviors. They tell themselves that something must have been wrong with them from the start. That they had something in their makeup that let them enjoy their abuse, and now they are sexually out of control in one way or another. Our brains and bodies are complex. My stance is that the abuser took control of a mental and physical system that was meant to give us pleasure. That it was the abuse that flipped that switch on too early, and there was no way anyone need feel guilty because someone else hijacked their sexual system. No guilt at all, but a burden to recognize this and work to break any promiscuous and inappropriate sexual behavior.

Sexual abuse can manifest itself whereby the victims become extremely disconnected from others and very lonely. They feel badly about themselves and their lives. Any spark of something positive can become something they cling to. There is a second or two of just physical release that is usually what drives these victims to different forms of sexual addiction. That second of release is the only bright spot in a day filled with confusion, guilt and shame. It is like chasing the high from a drug. If we're not "mindful" of our behavior, it is so easy to fall into this type of trap. The word mindful in the previous sentence is used to speak about a state of mind whereby the mind and body are in harmony. Harmony can only be achieved when we are happy of who we are—in other words, we like who we have become. I believe it is only in this state of mind that we can be involved in loving, caring relationships. Being mindful is being selfless in thoughts and deeds. I am certainly not the originator of this word or term, but I love to use it as an example.

Since most victims developed two of these behaviors or habits, here is a way to look at this uncomfortable subject:

If we are cut with a knife, but don't *want* to bleed, will that make a difference? Same with this, our bodies have been built to receive pleasure from sex. But what young child knows this? So those physical feelings of enjoyment become strong tides of guilt and shame and weave into so many other aspects of a person's life.

Looking back at myself, I do know that even though I was a young boy when it happened and even though I have studied and read and learned so much, I still have feelings of shame and guilt about the babysitter events of my past.

I'm not sure what I could have done differently.

No children are born bad. The world shapes us, mixes with our natural strengths and weaknesses; then our moral choices take form, and it all determines what we become. The acts I suffered at the hands of my mother and a teen babysitter were not only sexually inappropriate—they were flat out sadistic. Yet someone taught it to them. I wish we could all reach out, share the truth and break the cycle and heal all who have been affected.

What a nice dream, but I'll settle for this book helping just one person either deal with being abused or to recognize their behaviors and stop the pattern cold.

There is another almost hidden or overlooked aspect to severe abuse of any kind. It is called post traumatic stress disorder (PTSD). We have all heard this phrase in the news connected with soldiers coming back from the war. That is the headline grabber, what is of less interest to our media are adults who struggled with living a normal life due to childhood trauma. It must not be glamorous—I suppose it is embarrassing to highlight how poorly countless American children are treated.

The sad truth is that PTSD disrupts a person's life daily. Even if they are not experiencing a flashback (the Hollywood dramatic portrayal of PTSD), a person who suffers from this will plan their whole life around avoiding situations that could trigger a negative reaction. In addition to this, PTSD sufferers usually have difficulty sleeping and feel detached from life. Imagine not sleeping well...for twenty years! PTSD can actually change brain function and behavior because of the constant stress hormones flooding the body.

What this means to me and my siblings is that we have not only had to deal with the psychological damage from our outrageous childhood, but we have health (physical) problems that affect us all and add just one more layer of challenge that we have to overcome to work ourselves into a loving and fulfilling life.

CHAPTER 4

High School

*15% of all school absenteeism is directly related to
fears of being bullied at school.
Harassment and bullying have been linked to 75%
of school-shooting incidents.
Students shoot others because they have
been victims of physical abuse at home.*

—National Education Association

I promptly suppressed the memories of any sexual abuse; my best guess is that I did it immediately. I still couldn't get away from the fact that daily verbal and physical abuse was still erupting in our house. What I do know is that I spent every spare moment I could somewhere else. For all of my teen years, I found anything and everything to do that would keep me from being home.

Life was just a little different back when I was in high school. I attended Germantown High School in Philadelphia in 1969 and 1970. The school was a war zone with gang members actually attending school between fights. I took metal shop one semester and actually watched two students build a zip gun! As incredible as it sounds, it happened. Fear at home and fear at school! I'm sure most of these people have long since passed; however, they instilled real fear in me at the time.

Boy, almost every aspect of my life fit in like boxes being checked off when I run down the issues abused kids' exhibit today. The only box I wouldn't check would be drug use, well not hard drug use. My choice of drugs was marijuana. It just slowed my mind from 140 mph to 85 mph. For some reason, that became my medication. Over the years, I have been prescribed cocktails of just about every antidepressant, benzodiazepine, and antipsychotic medication known to man. In the final analysis, I have been on 75 mg of Venlafaxine for the past twelve years. In combination with this, I take 0.5 mg or 1 mg of Alprazolam at bedtime for sleep. Unfortunately, without medication, I just couldn't sleep. I believe it was directly related to the abuse that was worse at night when everyone was home and vulnerable. This combination helped stabilize my mood and kept me on a level field.

I got a job at a gas station as soon as I was able. People didn't pump their own gas back then, and with every full tank someone purchased, I would hear, "Fill 'er up, Bucky." We would be expected to wash down the front and back windows while the tank was being filled. My nickname back then was Bucky. I don't remember how I got it, but it seemed decent enough to me, and it felt nice, like I was being accepted when people used it. The sound of the ding as a car ran over the hydraulic line, the smell of the gas and wiper fluid; I really enjoyed all of that.

The gas station work wasn't hard at all; I did enjoy the superficial joking around with the drivers, and it felt really nice when returning customers would remember my nickname. I also enjoyed the fact that my pals could come over when I was working and hang around and talk to me. When I wasn't clocked in, I would just hang out there as long as my friends could stand it.

It wasn't long after my fifteenth birthday when I brought the physical abuse to an end.

It had been three years since I had been sexually molested, yet during those three years, I was still beaten down by physical and verbal assaults. Nevertheless, I was growing into an adult man. While my father may have taken the onslaughts of verbal abuse, he was not physically abused like we were. Ann may have slapped or punched him occasionally, but he did not suffer being beaten with objects like we did. I did not want confrontation, but I had been building up anger and also a wall. I wasn't going to take being beaten for much longer.

It was a lovely day in mid-spring. The day was just calling to me with a light breeze and temps in the seventies. I decided to skip school. I actually skipped school a lot and still managed to keep very passable grades as I mentioned. This was a perfect day that I just couldn't resist. I skipped school and went to my uncle's house for a quiet afternoon. My uncle never questioned why I skipped school although he knew the reputation of Germantown High at the time.

Later that evening, I had been home for a while, pretending that I had had a regular day. I ended up in my parent's room using their electric typewriter for a school assignment. I had never used the typewriter before, so I was concentrating on the keys and even peeking under my fingers every so often to make sure I was hitting the right letters. You had to really press or smash down hard to make the typewriter throw its arm forward and stamp your letter on the paper. So I was more or less hunched forward, and my ears were filled with the sound of the keys hitting the paper.

My mother came into the room.

"Mike, did you go to school today?"

"Yes," I said without hesitation or thought, said it nice and casual. Hey, I had played that game before and not been caught.

Whap! A slap across the face.

"Liar!" she shouted, leaning down to get almost nose to nose with me.

I launched myself to my feet. I had instantly decided to end her life. I had never lost control of my temper before, but I was now totally out of control. She must have sensed something was about to happen, something was dangerously different about what was going on now and even she could pick up on it. We had locked eyes. She began to back away from me. But the way we had been when this confrontation started out, this meant that she was not backing out the bedroom door but backing away from and deeper into the room—into a corner. I stood frozen but murderous for a second or two. Our eyes were still locked. Then I began to stalk her into that corner. I must have been puffed out with tension and hatred. I could feel my fingers twitching, getting ready to strangle her to death.

"David! David! Get the hell in here NOW!"

She still didn't break eye contact with me. I think if she had, I would have sprang on her. That would have been her last day on earth.

I was still stalking forward when my father's hands wrapped around my upper arms, locking them together behind me and pulling me backward out of the bedroom. My whole body was stiff, and my heels scrapped on the floor as I was pulled out. I had not moved my eyes from hers yet.

"If you *ever* put a hand on me again, I will kill you," I said that low with a snarl.

She never did.

My father struck me only a few times in anger throughout my whole life. It never hurt me, just frightened me because of the rarity of it. The last time my father tried to hit me, I was probably twelve. As he went to hit me, I ducked, and he hit his hand on a dresser that was double stacked. He bruised his hand badly. He just mentioned the other day (some forty-nine odd years after the fact) that he still has residual pain from hitting the dresser. Oh well.

Back to my career in truancy.

I found high school to be pure torture as well as having to endure an intolerable home life. The high school issue wasn't unique to me; we lived in Philadelphia and the high school for the area we lived in was predominantly black. I never fit in, and in the seventies, there was a much more rigid racial divide. There was violence in the school every day. Some of the violence was racial, but a greater part of it was general gang-type violence, and it was a daily occurrence; it happened to include all the quiet white kids but was as bad for the quiet black kids too. In two years, I don't think I ever ate lunch in the school cafeteria; it was downright dangerous there. The cafeteria was located in the basement of the school, and word was that you may go down and not come back up. With all I had witnessed in other parts of the school, I believed it, and since I was not part of a gang, I could travel with; I did not go down there.

I usually ate in the back room at a local bar with some other friends from school. The owner of the bar knew how bad it was in that school, and he let us use his room. I remember he even let us drink his soda. Angels do visit the world—I would like to honor that man who owned Frank's Bar and Grill in the late sixties and seventies. That act of quiet kindness certainly saved many broken bones and bruises, but it also certainly kept a group of boys from going over to the dark side, as I am sure we would have had to do for survival if we didn't have that haven to rest in.

We all really can find some small thing we can do to make the world a better place. Share a little room for lunch, share a smile or share whatever you can spare.

I was never one for any confrontations, home life was volatile enough. If I found myself in a situation that seemed to be heading toward some macho fight as an ending, I would just fade away to another part of the school. In my early years, I attended Howe Elementary School, which was located at Broad and Olney in

Philadelphia. At the time (late fifties and early sixties), there was a system of testing that could promote kids either a half or full grade: such as 4A or 4B. I believe that I skipped the entire second grade—going from first to third. So I was a year younger than most of the kids in my class. That set me up for being the smallest kid in my class, which—in that tough school—led to my being robbed, assaulted, threatened, and intimated every day for two years. I now believe that pushing me ahead in that skip period was just another hurdle, which left me on an uneven playing field.

Sigh. Boy, it's good to be alive!

Yet looking back, I think I also felt emotionally younger than most of my classmates. No, I know it. And in fact, being honest with myself, I was emotionally slow to mature and never really matched my physical age until I was in my forties. It was then that I finally began to feel settled into myself and a life I was creating. That is right, can you believe it? In my forties. Then I had nearly twenty plus wonderful years and a wonderful life full of friends and family. There is always a reason to keep working on ourselves.

All through my early adulthood, I was still ruled by my suppressed pain, shame and anger; anger that a difficult school situation only made my situation worse. Funny that I never labeled it as "anger." I never really took the time to think about it as it was all rolled up with suppressing the bad memories. Yet I was touchy, quick to yell and very unforgiving of anything I felt was "done to me" by my friends.

I recall that in my junior year, I would attend school on Monday, Tuesday and Wednesday and skip Thursday and Friday. In hindsight, attending three days a week must have been enough for me to retain what information I needed in order to pass my exams, and skipping a whole grade meant I was not a dummy, yet I always felt out of place and never connected to learning in school.

Things were so bad that I opted to join the Air Force and head for Vietnam rather than stay at home after high school.

The Vietnam War was the first to be televised. Americans would gather around the one TV set in the living room to watch the evening news and hear the latest action. It was alarming that I was now able to watch napalm bombs explode over the jungle and see the bodies of dead American soldiers being dragged to rescue helicopters.

I could have joined the Army, but even back then, I had a little swagger growing in my personality and wanted a little glamour in my life. I wanted to have that sharp uniform and be connected to powerful aircraft. All the better that this coolness would be gained while marching straight to my death. So I enlisted in the Air Force—thinking that being part of darting into and out of the thick of things, being around pilots and the awesome machines they flew—all this would be exciting and well worth dying for as some kind of hero.

This will be argued by anyone in any other branch of the military, but I think those dark blue dress uniforms really looked sharp.

CHAPTER 5

Good Morning, Philippines

Approximately 2/3 of assaults are committed by
someone known to the victim.
38% of rapists are a friend or acquaintance.

—*rainn.org/statistics*

The war had been front and center in American lives for over three years. I had volunteered to fight in Vietnam right out of high school.

Thinking back on that time of my life, it brings to mind that movie with Robin Williams, *Good Morning, Vietnam*, and I relate to many aspects of it. The bustle, the camaraderie. Light work for the most part, beautiful country all mixed with some dangerous assignments and stretches with no rest, then back to light work.

I was prepared to enlist and go off and fight and die. I had no anchors, no joy in life. I had one good friend and family members I never wanted to see again. No money, no higher education, no marketable skills and no game plan. There was not much to look upon and feel good about. When I enlisted, I volunteered for Vietnam just to get the hell out of my "home" and let the world decide. Who rolled those dice? The roll went my way. I did not fight in the thick of the jungle and die; my military orders took me to the Philippines. I was both relieved and disappointed. Relieved I did not have to be located in the midst of constant battle; I detested fighting of any kind. Disappointed because something inside of me wanted to die, just did not feel worthy of a decent life.

Like so many other people with an abusive childhood, I could not visualize how I could ever create an existence I saw as "normal" from the wreckage that I lived in. Therefore, I was going to play fast and loose with my life.

When I reached the Philippines, I really got to let a hidden light of mine shine through. I had seen glimmers of this passion of mine when I worked pumping gas and had brief and enjoyable superficial talks with the drivers. I had been so busy hiding from school and home violence that I had no time to really explore what I thought of people in general. People who were strangers to me and would never have the chance to get close to me and therefore hurt me in some way. What I found was that people fascinated me. Looking at it from where I am today, perhaps that is not so unusual. Many people who have been abused turn out to be advocates in some way for those who are being oppressed. For me, the camaraderie and positive relationships with other airmen were extremely fulfilling. It was like learning to breathe again.

First off, Clark Air Base was very different from Philadelphia. As you entered through the main gate, a large basic white sign was about forty feet above with black lettering: CLARK AIR BASE. No confusion there. A flat tin roof stretched over the booth/cabin where the guards stayed. The roof hung out over both sides—covering the entrance and exit. Light poles and chain link fences finished it all off. That was pretty…well…uninspiring.

As you drove in past the main gate, it was of course very flat where the flight line was—there were jet fighters and cargo planes that used the runway constantly. The fun thing for me was that palm trees were growing all over the base. It was tropical, and I witnessed some of the prettiest sunrises and sunsets that you can imagine. The soldiers were always relocating every few years, and this gave them the ability to make instant friends to become a band of joking, positive clowns during off time that allowed me to feel like I was fitting in. Sure there was some macho posturing here and there, but it couldn't hold a candle to the violence that went on in my high school. Already I was feeling some burden lifted from my soul. (Now, I would never have said it that way back then, all I knew then was that I actually woke up in the mornings and looked forward to what that day was going to hold—something I never did when at home.)

I was not interested in going to the NCO club and downing drinks until I staggered home. That was fine if you liked it. I was too leery of not being in complete control of myself—too afraid a drunken condition could lead to me regret losing control. That is how I rationalized my choices back then. Remember I had repressed all the memories of sexual abuse and even most of the physical abuse. I had to have some conscious reason to give me hope. I settled for what appeared to be my perception that I was in "control," which was true—just not the whole truth.

I also was not interested in sitting around the barracks and playing poker or reading or whatever. What sparked my interest was learning about local life. I wanted to get to know what the people were like. To know what their average days were like as well as their special festivals, holidays, or birthdays (more on why this fascinated me later). I knew I could not learn this on the base, I had to get out there into the surrounding little town called Angeles (village sounds condescending—and that was not the spirit I was in when I ventured forth). I also couldn't just wander down the main street, hit all the shops set up just for GI's, interact only with people that made their living off military personnel because those people were acting in a way they thought they should for an American.

No. I had to walk off base and go down the road that our leaders told us not to go down. Sure, it was that fabled *road less traveled*, still it *was* actually dangerous to wander around like that; the Philippines were under very strict martial law in the seventies. The penalty for many crimes was death, and executions went on regularly during the few years I was there. I felt a thrill rush through me as I walked far enough that I could no longer see the gates to the military base. I was on my own now. What was going to be in store for me?

Some of the best memories of my life. Like so much in my life when I just go for it with a spirit of love and calmness. Moreover, this first adventure helped that little spark of love for people to grow stronger.

The main street was about three miles with small alleys darting in all directions. The broad street was both macadam (black top) and dirt. The street was flat with black top in the middle, but the sides were dirt, and all the alleys were dirt. Shops and businesses lined both sides of the street, clustered very close together around the base for about three miles, but about a mile out on each side of the gate, they slowly morphed and had a little more room. By clustered, I mean they all shared a common wall and even the homemade signs crushed against each other—causing a cacophony of visual input for your eyes. These buildings were and cluttered and tattered, and barely structurally sound.

Everything was kin to the dust. Yes, there were a few palm trees around, but the buildings were concrete or old light-colored bricks. The dust settled in a film on everything. The signs were mostly white with red lettering. The only colorful sights were the women.

Again, close to the base the shops were mostly bars, music played constantly streaming out of the open doors to the bars. They had names like The Libra, DMZ Bar or just BAR. They really looked like they do in our movies…cracking cement walls, latticed bamboo wood for windows and railings—all in such disrepair that it would be condemned in the U.S., but they were bustling there. Also streaming out of the bars with the music were four to six women at each place; they were all displaying their wares and asking the GIs to rent them (pay their bar fine) for thirty-five pesos ($5.00). These were mostly very lovely women, tanned and light brown skin, deep sparkling eyes and that awesome straight black hair. Some were wearing very short dresses; some wore jean shorts and tied tops. This was not hidden behavior; these were legal, legitimate businesses. There was one place right across from the gate where the women were standing, openly waiting for a GI to come along and slip into a back room. It was like a dream for me initially: so many women and so little time. I started making up for my lack of love in the wrong way. That type of promiscuous "love" was short-lived and was not meaningful past the moment.

What really has had long-lasting influence on me was the other type of adventure with people who lived outside of Angeles.

There I was, strolling down a street where no one spoke English, looking very white and out of place. From behind, a kid smacked into me; he must have been about eight or ten. He was playing with a flattened soccer ball; because it was flat, he really had to kick it with vigor to get it to go. So I got his head crammed into my hip; he must have been leaning forward to deliver one of those kicks. He looked up at me with a crooked grin, a grin that didn't need any translation. Since I smiled back at him, he decided to kick his ball alongside of me as I kept walking. He would occasionally pluck at my shirtsleeve; it was a basic blue shirt made of cotton. Nothing special to me, but different from what most of the locals had to wear. At this time of harsh martial law in the PH (Philippines), all military personnel were to wear civilian clothes when off base. Even so, we were white or black skinned, and our clothes gave us away in less than a second. This kid knew he had head butted an American by accident, but he was curious and happy and tugging on my shirt in a playful, teasing way.

I then tugged at his dirty white tank top. He laughed. I smiled. As we neared what I was later to find out was his house, I smelled some delicious spices warming the air and my nose. He noticed me sniffing and just nodded. I was clueless, but as the kid cut off the street and headed toward the open doorway, he plucked my sleeve again, tugging me off the middle of the street and toward the house with him. Before I caught my balance, there was his mother, frowning at him. A lovely woman, thin with long black hair and an orange shift dress. She must have thought her son was in trouble, seeing a GI towering over her son, and it must have looked like I was escorting him home. That would only happen if the boy had gotten into some kind of trouble. There was a look of worry on her face, and she took hold of him by the shoulders, pulling him closer to her.

There was no way I could have gotten out of staying for dinner. Mom was now smiling at me and nodding back, though I had not spoken a word she could understand, and frankly, I was trying to avoid eye contact with her. Like moms everywhere, once she decided you were coming to dinner, you better get with the program and not give her any flack. The dad was already sitting at the wooden table; then we joined him and a younger daughter. They couldn't speak English, and I couldn't speak Tagalog. Somehow, we had fun. They would shove something at me; we would all take a bite of the same dish, and they would lean forward to soak in my reaction to their food. It didn't matter if I made a yummy sound, gave a puckered look or waved the so-so sign. They would smile and put another taste on my chipped, thick white plate. They would also say the name of what we were eating, and I would parrot it back to them, much to their amusement.

They were living in what we would call abject poverty, yet they were happy and generous and truly great hosts. I had nothing to offer them in return, but they seemed pleased to receive hugs and waves. I left them smiling, and I was also grinning widely. Wow. What a rush to have a family dinner that was filled with human kindness.

Over my year and a half there, I had many similar connections to the people that lived there but were not connected to the base. What I mean by this is that there were many local people who made their living doing jobs that served the American military there. The area was famous for its wicker and monkey pod wood items. Nearly all the soldiers would buy and ship some of the furniture home. Some shops had a little area out front where they would actually be making the furniture, weaving the wicker or shaping the monkey pod wood as us Americans would watch. They would stack finished items on top of each other, and most got pretty high and looked like something from Dr. Seuss which was crooked and about to tumble down on my head. These people were very nice, but they were totally geared toward making Americans feel comfortable, so they could make a sale. They learned catchphrases and could speak basic English.

I sought after people who never had to interact with an American. I guess I thought of them as more authentic, not spoiled by Americans. I made it a hard and fast practice to always head off base during my free time and strike out in a new direction. But now, I carried candy bars and hard candy to give to any pleasant people I might run into. Just a small kind of gift, money would have been an insult, but a small bit of candy—who could refuse that?

Another aspect of my time here was my promiscuousness, which I mentioned briefly earlier. It is a typical behavior manifested by those who have been sexually abused. What happens is that having sex with strangers is a release, a way to relax physically and to have a connection with other humans that is controlled and not threatening. But it is all superficial, though this is never realized at the time.

As soon as a friendship or warmth would start to develop with any woman I was having sex with, it would bring up the feelings in me of betrayal and pain, and I would push that woman away and look for a new one. In other words, as soon as any affection would bloom, that was the end because feelings of fear and shame and anger would all be swirling just under the surface of my mind. I was not ready to deal with any of that. Let alone have something like affection turn into love! Love that was dangerous and couldn't be counted on for anything. Oh no. I was staying as far away from that as I could get.

So that "relationship" would end and on I would go to the next stranger. Having repressed the memories of abuse, I had no idea why I was moving from girl to girl. I chalked it up to being a young man and thought no more of it. Plenty of servicemen were bragging about their sexual encounters, so I felt almost as if I were finally fitting into the rest of society.

My time in the PH was coming to a close. It was January of 1975, and I was taking a last stroll down Angeles' main street. Crammed next to the bars and wicker stores were vendors with barbecue chicken flavoring the air. I breathed it all in. Listening to the chicken gizzards sizzle and feeling the hot sun on my face. A loud rumble went by and replaced the savory meat smell with diesel. It was a jeepney, what served as taxis in the PH. They were pieced together from old WWII jeeps left behind in various states of decay. Now they were decorated with taxi names and letterings and odd paint combinations. The one that just went past was bright yellow and orange with words in red.

In addition to these Frankenstein-type taxis was the bus transportation called the Rabbit. I had often grabbed a ride into Manila for under $4.00 to hit the nightlife in the "big city." Manila was the place to go for nightclubs and the feel of a decadent urban area. Not only Americans, but also the local people all headed to Manila when they wanted the taste or feel of an urban area. Still, it was a dangerous place to play in; many muggings and fights would break out every single night in the big city. Mostly when we went, we went in groups for our city fun.

But no rides for me this afternoon. I turned back and strolled for the gate, time to pack it up and catch my plane home. Thanks to the USAF and the Philippines I had received some time to just be, just to go about living a day and refresh myself. I had seen some functioning and loving families. I had days of good fellowship with the guys. I had started to look forward to the days each morning when I woke up. I still had no grand plan for life, but now, I had a little more energy and a much better outlook on what life could be.

CHAPTER 6

You Are My Sunshine

54% of sexual assaults are not
reported to the police
97% of rapists will never spend a day in jail.

—rainn.org/statistics

I decided to take advantage of a program called the GI Bill to go to college after I got out of the Air Force; they paid for college, and I think a small amount to live on. I also held down a part-time job at a service station, so I was bringing in steady money; not great, but steady, and I was doing okay for a single young man.

I was sitting in class one day when I looked over and noticed Robin for the first time. At that time, not long since I left the military, I took some joy in letting my hair go…this included facial hair. I must have been a sight with my dark watchman's cap, black hair that was wavy and well below my ears (for back then, that was nigh on being a rebel) and thick facial hair. I wonder if anybody could actually see any of my facial expressions at all. Some say now I look a little like Robert De Niro—so that gives you a basic idea of what my facial features are like and even more so how unkempt I must have looked in class. (If you go to the back of the book and find the picture of my grandfather Leo—I look almost exactly like him.)

So there I was, looking over at this lovely co-ed—quiet, smart, and she just took my breath away. I'm not saying this to put something sweet in print—I knew I wanted to marry her. Bam! Just like that. And the more I learned about her and listened to her talking in class, the surer I was about it.

She was everything the women in my past were not…quiet, helpful, friendly. I quietly watched her for weeks, soaking in everything she said and did. She was vivacious, having fun with life. She could go from very conservative to wearing a headband and spiking up her hair; I thought she looked as gorgeous and very much like Olivia Newton-John. In fact, she looked a lot like Olivia back then physically and style wise. Now we may look back at those pictures and laugh at the styles, but at the time she was cutting edge, giving a balance to conservative and spunky. And I loved the mix! Slender with thick light brown hair. Her waist was so small I was sure I could circle it with just my hands. She still has high, strong cheekbones which keep her looking tall and young. Combining both the boldness and kindness of her personality with perfect looks, there was no way I was ever going to be able to live without her.

I knew I couldn't take any rejection from her—she was **IT** for me. So I began to take stock of the situation.

First, I had to get out of my antifashion rut, at the very least clean up.

Check.

Nice haircut, shave and ditch the watchman's cap.

Check.

Clean jeans and a decent shirt.

Check.

Now what? I let a few more weeks go by. Always noticing her and how she behaved. She was grace and elegance. I hadn't changed my mind about her. Still, I knew that if I did not approach her in the right way, I could blow my chance. But I couldn't wait forever. Yet I was still afraid because I felt my future hinged on her accepting me; therefore, I couldn't say anything stupid or anything that would cause her to shut the door on me.

So one day as were walking in the main entrance of the building, I went up to her and asked if I could talk to her after class.

"Sure."

Okay, not much to go on, but it was sort of a yes.

"Okay, I'll meet you here after class."

"K."

Robin says that she had noticed me before and thought I looked good but scruffy. Then when I got myself cleaned up while getting ready to make my move on her, she says she noticed that too, and she and a girlfriend of hers said to each other, "Gee, he cleans up nice." So I guess I had a better chance than I thought. I never knew they were paying any attention to me.

She says she got an actual physical head rush when I finally asked to talk to her after class and then told herself, "Well, no. He probably just wants my notes from English class. Don't even think that he wants to go on a date."

So maybe it wasn't love at first sight in a love-struck kind of way, but it sure was a feeling in both of us that this was the right person, right from the start. I really get a kick out of knowing I was so scared and knew I just couldn't blow this first date…while *she* was tingling from the toes up to her head in the hopes that I was going to ask her on a date. How wonderful is that? What a magnificent human moment.

Dating was great. We got along so well, and it just confirmed to me that this was the one for me. She was the first girl I was letting get really close to me. Before this, I would always keep girls at a distance. Sure I would take them to dinner or buy them a little something, but never got close. I had never confided in a girlfriend or depended on them for anything at all. Robin was different, and it was all going so well. I started to relax, and those fears that came with affection were fading away while Robin was shining on. After about four months of dating Robin, an incident occurred which meant nothing to me at the time.

Robin bought me a shirt and tie as a gift. She bought the wrong-sized shirt. It was half a size off. This is what I handed her.

"If you cared about me, you would know the right size of shirt to buy me."

What a payback for a gift! A hefty dose of guilt mixed with some verbally abusive tones and facial expressions. I didn't see it that way, and after the dust settled down that day, I went back to being a loving boyfriend. It just doesn't get any more classically abusive than that! But I didn't see it, Robin didn't see it, and society was not as open with calling attention to the dark side of human nature yet. Most of us were under the false impression that every person was either a good person or a bad person. Our brains just didn't compute that there could be a healthy mixture of both in a decent human being.

So we didn't recognize it as a pattern of human behavior. We thought it was a bump in the road; we made up and moved on.

Julie, her mother, had a better handle on me and did not like me at all. I believe she thought I was cocky, controlling and manipulative and all topped off with a big chip on my shoulder. Julie was right. But I had a handle on her too; she was just as controlling as I was.

I knew Robin was my true love but did that mean I was also marrying my in-laws? They were not going to control me. I already had all the craziness I needed. I'd be damned if I was going to be put down by anyone else.

Ah, the first date. It was still common to "meet the parents" of a girl when going on a first date. I remember Bob, Robin's father, was in the kitchen painting the walls. He would not even come into the living room to meet me. "How strange," I thought to myself.

Robin says I was young and belligerent, and she can understand why they didn't like me. I suppose that is pretty right on. I do know I made an effort to be courteous, but I will admit that I may have *said* the right words, but I can only imagine my tone and body language were singing a different tune.

The clashes and angst came from the other side too. Ann was never nice to Robin. She was always short and very bossy whenever we would visit. When we showed our engagement ring to my parents, they just said, "That's nice." It seemed they did not care for Robin one way or the other, nor were they happy for us. It was like I just told them I was going out for a burger and fries.

The disinterest of my family was like a slap in the face. Even though I had run from home straight to the military to get away, they were still my family, and I always wanted their love and approval. Even after all the hell, I guess we are hardwired to love our parents.

The engagement announcement did have a better reception with Julie and Bob. I guess they looked at it as a done deal and were now going to make the best of it. Julie also loved to plan a party, so she and Robin were off and running with wedding plans. Finally, a little give on that side.

Today, I describe Bob as a really good man; he is almost eighty years old. We try to set up dinners whenever we can. Julie and I get along well, and we so very much enjoy holidays when we all get together. The three of us almost hated each other at first. It started out rough, and I felt the tension every time I had to be in the presence of my in-laws. Now…I wouldn't trade them for anything—I love 'em too much! They really have been there for us, the kids and the grandkids. They have been there in ways that were missing when I was a child, and I didn't even know it.

I can tell you our lives are enhanced because of them. Here is a great example: special occasions. My family was basically disowned by my grandparents because my dad did not raise us in the Orthodox Jewish faith. That is not the only thing my parents didn't do. We did not celebrate birthdays—no parties, cakes or candles. It was just another day for us. Even if we were not practicing Orthodox, we could have celebrated Hanukkah and had those eight nights of little presents! No. Nothing. Nothing was special or happy or joyous about life in that household. Robin and her family introduced some wonderful traditions into my life.

One very special time of sharing that has carried on is the birth of each of our children and now our grandchildren. When Chad was born, Robin's grandmother, Julie's mother, came and stayed with us for ten days or so to help Robin with the new baby. She had a very hard labor and delivery and needed the help. As Julie had young children of her own and worked, Lena, or Gram as we called her, packed her bag and stayed with us. Robin and I both have wonderful memories of that time. She came with all three babies. Now all these years later, Julie packed her bag each time our daughter Lindsay had a baby. Of course, Robin and I helped as much as we could, but we both work full time. Just like Robin and her grandmother, Lindsay has grown to cherish this time with her grandmother. And Julie loves it too. As a great grandmother, she has bonded so greatly with these four little babies. What a gift!

Bob is a very religious man. He raised his children in the Lutheran faith, and to my knowledge, none of them ever missed a week of church unless they were sick. All five children went to catechism classes and were active in the church's youth group. As staunch a Christian as my father in law is, he never once voiced any objections to his daughter marrying a Jewish man. He IS a true Christian in that regard. His only concern was that his children are well loved and cared for. He would have been just as supportive if we decided to raise our children Jewish. He even said he would rather have them raised in the Jewish faith than no faith at all.

Now imagine the poor Orthodox side of my family realizing I was marrying a practicing Christian! Ah, I love it.

So now Bob teases me saying, "I never met a Jewish person that loves Christmas more than you do."

So true. I hold back nothing for Christmas. The house is decorated inside and out. We make sure all the presents are wrapped in matching colors or bows. I go in for all the wonderful Christmas songs playing all day long. The whole shebang. Robin has taught me well.

Holiday celebrations are traditions that Robin's family has shared with me. I delight in telling everyone I know, "Happy Birthday." Holidays and special occasions are big with us. Of course, the kids just love it, and that is so satisfying to me. For Easter, some twenty people plus their kids come over, and Robin serves delicious food she has prepped for days. This is a gang of brothers, sisters, wives, husbands, cousin, aunts and uncles. All getting along, all having fun. Can you see it? A gang of various family members getting along and sharing a celebration. My heart can barely contain the happiness. I videotape it all now. I just can't help myself.

This is part of the sunshine that Robin has brought into my life. **I LOVE YOU ROBIN.**

Some of the darkest days were to come, but we did have a perfect wedding a good running start at our adult life.

CHAPTER 7

Keep Your Head on a Swivel

I want to articulate a common behavior connected to my unbearable childhood and my character in the tales of the dark days to come, I wanted to include a little something about hypervigilance. This is a physical state a body comports in which all the senses are on high alert and overactive. I have read voluminous material on this topic, yet the definition that puts it all out there for the general public is the Wikipedia definition:

> Hypervigilance is an enhanced state of sensory sensitivity accompanied by an exaggerated intensity of behaviors whose purpose is to detect threats.
>
> Hypervigilance is also accompanied by a state of increased anxiety which can cause exhaustion. Other symptoms include abnormally increased arousal, a high responsiveness to stimuli, and a constant scanning of the environment for threats. In hypervigilance, there is a perpetual scanning of the environment to search for sights, sounds,

people, behaviors, smells or anything else that is reminiscent of threat or trauma. The individual is placed on high alert in order to be certain danger is not near.

This can lead to a variety of obsessive behavior patterns as well as producing difficulties with social interaction and relationships. Hypervigilance can be a symptom of PTSD and various types of anxiety disorders.

Sounds bad. Affecting health, behavior and interactions with people. I do not want to kid you; I still have the exhaustion and quick responses that come with hypervigilance. It did affect the ways I interacted with my business partners, neighbors and certainly my in-laws. It has had many negative effects on my life and my health. In my opinion, the most important often-misdiagnosed issue is the relationship between this particular behavior and the changes in brain chemistry that occur over time under this type of stress. Sadly, I believe the chemical changes that occur are irreversible and need to be supplemented by medications currently available. However, I do love to make lemonade out of a batch of shit. Here are three stories of how I used this as an asset and even for some fun occasionally.

How can this be an asset?

Robin and I were on our first tropical vacation, an island in the Caribbean. This was before all the current development, probably twenty-five years ago. On this island, there was a small "resort" area with a marketplace nearby and then the wild island where we were warned not to wander. The whole resort consisted of an average hotel, swimming pool, bar area and section of the beach. So not as glamorous as a resort vacation today, but still full of island beauty.

It was our last day of vacation; we were in the market area near the resort. I was on alert for pickpockets. I would have been anyway, but the hotel also warned all guests about this activity in the market-place. It was a typical bustling place with vending carts set up with wares from beers to veggies to jewelry. It was a little like the Old West with unpaved roads and shops all set up with stores on each side of the road.

Robin was a few steps in front of me as we shopped along the crowded streets. Ahead there were two men standing close—facing each other, yet on opposite sides of the middle of the path, people were walking back and forth between the two men. I immediately noticed one had his hand in his pocket—and that they were in a rather heated, not yelling yet, discussion. When people are angry, they usually waive their hands and become very animated, not keep a hand in their pocket.

I was on red alert. Just as Robin was walking between the two men, the one I was really watching pulled a knife out of his pocket. No one knew what was going on as I body tackled Robin to get her out of the way. We were both clear of those two men before any-one knew what happened. From a much safer distance, we watched as other local people controlled the man with the knife, and police showed up quickly.

I had reacted before I saw the knife, was moving Robin out of their range as it came out of his pocket. I was always under the impression this is hypervigilance, for the brain to recognize the signs that something is *going to happen* and react in enough time to be out of the way. I had been hurt enough in my life to learn those little facial and body tells that come right before someone erupts into action.

Therefore, in these types of situations, my hypervigilance saved us some bodily injury, if not death. That is a positive product of this terrible condition.

The next illustration is one out of thousands in my life. We are flashing forward many years into the future from the island incident. It is a winter night that got dark early with cold winter clouds hanging in the sky, making it really a deep dark night with the air on the edge of freezing rain. It was somewhere around eleven at night.

I saw a very large black man outlined in the dim light of a bus stop shelter. I pulled over to the curb and rolled down the passenger window.

"Hey, buddy. Wanna ride?"

His face was still as could be. "No. No, thank you. Bus is coming along soon."

I could see he was cold.

"I'm off work now, just going home. It is freezing. I'd love to give you a ride."

He still hesitated, but finally got in the car.

"Let's let the elephant out of the room—I am not afraid you are going to mug or kill me just because you are black. I saw you out there, you looked cold, and I would just like to give you a ride home. Where do you live?"

"Broad and Olney."

Ah, great—one of the worst parts of Philly, a white man driving a black man in this part of the city after dark. I smiled to myself.

What I said was, "Okay, I know that place. I grew up near there."

As we got closer, I could tell he was preparing for me to let him out at the outskirts of the bad area. I had no intention of that! By this time, we had talked a little, and I found out he was a chef in a very nice restaurant who just got finished work and going home to a place he could afford. I drove him right to his doorstep and wished him good night. I just have no fear of that type of thing. This is because I am really in tune with people and can pick out a person on the edge of violence in a heartbeat. I had him pegged as a decent man from the start. I do this often, some little ways that I find I can help people—they all thrill me. Moreover, because I can read danger (or lack thereof) in people, I just have no fear and wade right into situations.

Now for the most fun I had when scanning people and making a risky decision based on what my hypervigilance told me.

Back to that first vacation on that tropical island (not naming names because it is all built up now and may give you the wrong impression of the place back in the early eighties). While we slept at the resort each night, we went off by ourselves during the day. We were not interested in drinking all day and swimming in the resort pool—heck, we could do that at home. We wanted to explore and enjoy the tropical views and smells. We wanted to see different things.

The island was just beautiful, dotted with banana plantations and lush palm trees and vines everywhere. It was also where the harbor scene of Dr. Doolittle was filmed. Time to explore this lovely island. Good-bye, poolside chairs.

We walked to an isolated piece of beach well out of sight of our hotel and settled in. A few hours later, a man dressed in khaki shorts, a light cotton shirt and a floppy straw hat came strolling along the beach. He was a tall, lanky black man.

We waved and smiled. He waved back and said some sort of greeting. Then stopped and looked at us. I struck up a conversation with him. Little stuff like us being on our first vacation and enjoying the untamed nature of this quiet part of the beach. He said his name was George, and he was a resident of the island. When I came around to asking what he did, things got interesting.

"Live off the sea. You wanna go catch lobsters with me and my pals?"

"I'd love to catch lobsters!" I had no hesitation.

"You wait here. I'll be back."

He strolled off.

Robin was staring at me with her mouth open. Then she just shook her head at me.

A half an hour later, George showed up with two other tall black men; this time, his straw hat was off, and I saw dreadlocks hanging down to nearly his waist. How had he been able to tuck it all under that hat? It still makes me laugh when I think back on that day because I cannot believe all that hair fit under that hat.

The three of them were carrying a little boat out of the lush vegetation. As they strolled by our spot on the beach, I stood up and joined them, and we all walked to the surf, eased the little boat into the foam, I hopped in the boat with them and off we went.

Robin thought I was crazy—what if he was going to kill me or hold me for ransom. Maybe there were just islanders that hated Americans, and he was going to beat me up for sport.

Well, we paddled along and settled at a nice spot—we dove down and caught lobsters just like that! They certainly knew that spot well.

We came back onto the beach, built a fire and roasted lobster. We all sat around, ate, and talked. It was excellent. I said to myself, "Now this is living."

George made plans with us to meet the next day. We rented a car, and George took us exploring deep into the green island—where no tourist had gone before. The private tour (which George would not take money for) ended at a small trader stand on a high part of the island. This vendor's stand was in a very small marketplace with maybe six or seven other vendors. There were no towns around—just three of what the locals would have called roads in the near vicinity. I would have called them dirt paths. On this stand were set out some freshly baked pastries! I was expecting some type of vegetable or rabbit meat or noodles, right. No, the best pastries I had ever eaten.

I was able to meet an authentic islander, and with George as our personal guide, we really got to see this island in all its glory. We had the opportunity to enjoy the freshest lobster cooked in a way we had never thought of. Had the surprise of our vacation with pastry the French would have loved in the middle of the jungle. All because I just knew he was not a threat; I just knew he was exactly what he presented to me on the beach. I had not a doubt in my mind.

If 95 percent of the people I will meet and have met are fundamentally good people, what does that say? No matter who I am talking to if this topic comes up in conversation, I have an almost smug look on my face.

It means that 95 percent of people on this Earth are good. It is just that the others get all the media attention and even the family and community attention. I feel so optimistic about the future of our society and believe the world will be a good place for my grandkids to grow up.

I do not see humanity as being bad or evil, I see very few people being that way. Fortunately, I am able to pick them out (hypervigilant—seeing micro signals in the face and tension and tone of voice that other people may miss but that scream predator to me).

My children believe I was always the way people see me now, also most of my friends know me as I am now. I am normally a mellow person most days. Most days I smile and go out of my way to help friends and strangers alike. I guess that I really am that kind of guy now. However, what my kids and friends do not understand is that I did not lose the hypervigilance. I may look mellow, but inside, I am alert and tense. I may act mellow, but for most of my adult life, I was aggressive and not very pleasant to be around. They did not know the mean me, the one puffed up with anger and hurt. Even though my bad times are not obvious now, they are a permanent scar. It is just something within me all the time. It is like the people who have been through a concentration camp, never able to forget. Every time they see something with anti-Semitism, it takes them back to that horrible time in their lives. How do you get it out of their head? You never forget it. You grieve for it; you understand it—but it is always there. My hypervigilance is always there, like a program running in the background and using up energy constantly. It really can exhaust me some days.

Still, the majority of people I meet are good people.

I probably do something that includes reaching out in some way once a week. If not a ride, then a stop to help somebody change a flat. Nowadays, if somebody is stuck on the side of the road, people drive by if they do not know them. I cannot. If I see people in the car, and I am not sure how I feel about them—if they are safe or not—or I am late for something I can't put off, I'll pick up the phone and call 911 and say, "At mile marker 213 is a disabled vehicle."

What is so difficult about that? It is just going the extra step to help people. Isn't that in tune with humanity? Even my hypervigilance doesn't prevent me from helping in a dangerous situation. As somebody may say, "You picked up a black guy at night?"

I say, "Yeah, that's not the worst thing in the world."

Moreover, they may think I flirt with danger. I do not think I do. I think I live my life without that fear that maybe many people have and maybe my hypervigilance is something that guides me, but it is pretty much right on most of the time. My wife says, "How do you *know* that?" I just notice it, just something I pick up from intense observation.

Perhaps a personality trait of mine of just jumping right in to help total strangers started in the Philippines. They were happy there; the general people in Angeles City living in extreme poverty. I was amazed to see that with what little they had how happy they were. I was like, "Wow." They shared food with me, but more importantly, they shared kindness.

"YEAH! That's the stuff that I love!" I say it aloud as I think back to those humble, happy and poor people. Am I so amped up because it is what I never had as a boy? Perhaps. The reason does not make it less true and less powerful. This is how humans shine—kindness.

Yes, some people are a little arrogant. However, most people are not, and I know most people are good people. I am about to talk about my own period in life when I was tending toward snooty. A time when I was rude and sometimes outright nasty to others. I know it all stemmed from my own fear and pain. That is how I gladly deal with all people nowadays. I know that their bad behavior is a mask for pain and confusion and their own unhappiness.

CHAPTER 8

All Your Father's Fault

1 in every 10 rape victims are male.
2.78 million men in the U.S. have been vic-
tims of sexual assault or rape.

—National Institute of Justice & CDC & Prevention,
Prevalence, Incidence and Consequences
of Violence Against Women.

I had scored the woman of my dreams. Well, I had never even really dared to dream that such a wonderful person would appreciate me, let alone marry me. Yet, there we were—starting out our life together.

My subconscious must have been remembering a scene from my childhood, and this pushed me into the next phase of my life: obsession with money. When I was around nine or ten, Mom and Dad argued every day, as I mentioned. This particular day, Mom was in rare form and was nose to nose with Dad berating him while he stood in silence. As I was sliding by them to get to my room, she grabbed my arm. She swung me around so that I was between them and facing her.

"This is your father's fault. If he was a real man, he would get a better job, and then we would not have all these problems. Never be like your father. He cannot even support his family. What a failure."

She released me with a disgusted push.

My father never addressed that accusation, and it must have been a new one for me to hear, for it really snuggled down into my mind and quietly waited for the perfect time to resurface. It woke up when I had my own family to support; I was NOT going to be a failure. I was NOT going to be the cause of pain and anger within my family. Of course, since I equated success with money, I did fail, and I did cause pain and anger in my family. Fortunately, it was not of the same kind or intensity as I suffered. Also fortunately, it did not last for my kid's entire childhood and I found a different way to behave once my eyes were open to the truth of how I was really living and behaving.

My earliest memories of my dad were of a quiet, humble man. He was reliable and hard working. Since I did not have much interaction with him because he was always working, I never really bonded with him as a toddler or adolescent. Now that I think of things in this context, I do remember that he would stress the importance of money. Still, when I think of my father, I think of a man who was in the U.S. Navy (1951–1955) and was one of the first players on the newly formed navy soccer team. He worked hard all his life, worked for General Electric in the 1960s. Then he worked as a quality control inspector for the government. He retired in 2000 and has continued to reside in a modest two-story single home for the last forty years. He is eighty-six now and spends most days watching TV and playing with his cat. Most Sundays he come to our place for dinner and sees his girlfriend on the weekends. He still drives and is very physically active for his age. The cool thing for me is that he really likes Robin and believes she is a wonderful mother, which she is.

Back to starting out as a newlywed. I was in love, I wanted the best for Robin, and I was willing to work to get it. I worked with a vengeance—I was connected to Nationwide Insurance and determined to bring in top commissions for selling new policies. The first two years I got a basic salary, ongoing training, and commissions. This gave the new Nationwide agents time to build their business before they were switched to commission only. I had always been good at quickly relating to new people in a friendly way. This allowed me to communicate with my clients and really give them what they were looking for. My business grew very rapidly.

I remember we bought our first home in March of '79. It was the greatest feeling to be locking the door that night, having complete control of who entered our home. It was the first glimmer of a new feeling: it was the first time I started to feel safe in my entire life.

We were thrilled, and Robin was soon pregnant with our first child, Chad. Because I was making such good money, the plan was for Robin to quit her job and be a full-time mother. It was also much more the norm back in the early eighties, and we never questioned or thought about the possibilities of my falling on hard times. We were full speed ahead toward a perfect life.

I also partnered with a friend of mine, and we started a video rental store. That was way back when we all had those VHS tapes. Huge, clunky tapes that took up so much room, I have to laugh when I think about how unwieldy those things were. In addition, they tended to break easily, and then there was the issue of getting customers to rewind their tapes back to the beginning, so the next customer renting was not angry. You older readers remember those stickers on the tapes, Be Kind, Rewind. There was nothing worse than settling down with some popcorn and pressing play—and seeing the credits. That meant you had to rewind and sit there in silence for a few minutes. Pure torture, right?

In addition to Nationwide Insurance and the video store, I was a silent partner in a restaurant/bar located in University City right in Philadelphia. Like clockwork every Monday, my partner would hand me a wad of money. Life was good.

Working two jobs, filling in for employees who called in sick, managing stock and convincing people that home, life and auto insurance was for them, then occasionally doing something with the restaurant was my weekly routine. Then home to do my husband chores. Get up and do it again. Ah, the fun. It wasn't long before I was exhausted and neglecting Robin and our new son. I didn't see it that way, not yet. I did feel the money was coming in steady, and that was what gave me the false feeling that I was being a good husband and father. I was bringing in the money; our bills were paid, and we had money left over. Everything else was just a bump along the road.

Things started to get even better, my Nationwide agency was now much easier because I had established clients who were easy to deal with, and I would continue to earn commissions from the renewal of their policies. Any time I spent getting a new insurance client was like a bonus paycheck for me. I had now set up my own insurance agency; I was making about $150,000 per year in 1985, which is very good money now, but was a ton of money for that time.

I was soon at the point where I was overseeing the building of a custom home for Robin and I. I was there every day, coordinating and keeping all the contractors moving ahead. This was not a McMansion, but it was a large house on five acres, and it was innovative for its time. It was what I refer to as an executive house. We moved in during 1988. I was very proud of that house. Doesn't pride come before the fall? Hum.

It was not the type of pride in a job well done or of rearing wonderful kids. It was the type of pride that was fueled by having more of something than other people. It was a mean-spirited pride.

We can all take pride in a job we have done well. In addition, the superb work of others is just as valuable. Logically, we know that a superb job done by someone else does not diminish our own well-done job. That is the win-win scenario. I don't think there is anything wrong with that kind of pride. However, when I became proud that my house was bigger and proud that I had swankier things than other people had in their houses, when I became proud that my car was more expensive than my neighbors could afford, then that feeling was dependent on others not winning so that I could stand at the top.

This happened slowly, like cooking a frog—do it slow, bring the water from room temperature to boiling slow enough, and the frog just fades to sleep and dies. Robin and I were and are good people. However, we slowly got used to being at the top. We would pay for others in our family to come on vacation with us. We would go out to eat nearly every day. We would take multiple vacations. No real harm in this, but it was cumulative. After a year or so of living like this, our attitudes started to change a little. I think we looked down on others, thought their financial situation was solely their fault and pointed to some flaw in their character, or that they were not working hard enough. Our old friends faded away. Frankly, I think we were acting like real A-holes toward anyone who was not keeping up with us. If you were not richer than we were, I don't think we were much fun to be around. We lost the skill of relating to others, as we were caught up in what I now call the money trap, and money was no object for us then.

And was that enough?

No. It never is when you are running on that treadmill. I needed more money. The peculiar thing was we were only in that big house for six months when things started to take a turn for the worse—financially speaking.

Since real estate always seemed a safe bet, and I had just built one of the loveliest homes in the state, I thought I should buy a large tract of land and build ten new homes. Then sell them off at a huge profit. In order to pull this off, I had to use this lovely new house as collateral for the project. With the house as security, I was able to negotiate a huge loan for this project, well over a million dollars. The monthly interest payments were staggering—but I was successful at almost everything I worked at. I thought I had the Midas touch.

With one of the new homes completed and the next one starting, the economy slowed down (this would turn out to be the beginning of the recession). I could not sell the first house. Nevertheless, I had to sell the first house to continue building the other nine homes! I was anxious for months, worried that I might not sell this house and having no idea of what sort of deals I could make if that happened. I was trying to keep cool and keep my rising panic from Robin and the family. But I was nearly sick to my stomach, while at the same time, my mind was racing trying to come up with things I could do that would get the bank to forgive my loan. I was coming up empty, and time was racing away from me.

At the last possible moment, we got a buyer for the finished house. I almost collapsed in relief, one down and nine to go. We started working again on the next lot—house no. 2. I had a taste of fear, and I did not like it, so I threw myself into the project. I was convinced my hard work would make it happen.

As the months ticked on, all my savings were drained paying just the monthly interest. I was not even touching the principal amount of that huge loan. Now the pressure really started. The bankers and attorneys were relentless at meetings I had to attend, trying to promise anything I could so that they would extend the loan or forgive a month's interest payment. Finally, it boiled down to no good solutions. I could not sell the next house. Construction had come to a standstill. As time went on, there was nothing else I could promise or do to satisfy the bank's fears.

We were going to have to declare bankruptcy to get out from under the loan and the building project. This meant we were going to lose the home I had built just for Robin. The home we planned to live in for the rest of our lives.

As part of the bankruptcy agreement, I was able to make a deal for a very small nest egg amount of $20,000, which I was going to use for rent payment or as a down payment for a smaller home. In turn, the bank was able to take complete control of the project, and subsequently, I was out.

We lost the huge tract of real estate, my credit was ruined, and we had to be out of our grand home and turn it over to the bank shortly, and at this same time, the district manager from Nationwide Insurance phoned to schedule an appointment to discuss my future with Nationwide. It turned out, that the company claimed that I ran an unprofitable agency and had twelve months to improve my loss ratio, or my contract with the company would be terminated.

What?

I was going to be homeless in a month. Now jobless too? Homeless because we would have to be out of the big house in one month, and no bank would approve a mortgage since we had just filed for bankruptcy.

Robin put her foot down at this time. "I just don't want to rent again." Pause.

Her head was down, concentrating on wrapping up glasses. "I don't want to move the kids out of the area; it's hard for kids to move around, and the school is really good. Why is this happening to us?"

She looked up from the boxes she had been packing. Packing because we had to be out of there, but we had no place to go. The oldest of our three kids was ten. Tears were shimmering in her eyes. She was trying hard to be brave but was still angry and scared of the unknown future. I had been running too hard, too fast and too hot. Now we were broken down at the side of the road with nowhere to go.

What were we going to do?

CHAPTER 9

Anger Issues

*In homes where one parent perpetrates violence
against the other, children are abused at a rate
1500% higher than the national average.*

—National Coalition Against
Domestic Violence, Washington D.C.

*Boys who grow up in homes where violence
is occurring are **100 times more likely**
to become abusers.*

—Victims of the System (Washington
D.C.: U.S. Senate Committee
on the Judiciary

*A history of child abuse increases a person's
likelihood of being arrested by 53%.*

—Penn State University

I'm going to leave Robin on the floor packing our belongings for now and go back to those years of wealth because the money didn't make those years perfect. Some of the days were just wonderful, full of kids, fun, and kisses. Some of the days were horrible, full of my anger, tantrums, and fear of losing the material possessions I was working so hard to keep.

I was always happy to come home at the end of the day. I would play with the kids and eat dinner with the whole family. Then have a little quiet time in the house with Robin once they were off to bed. If I came home late, it was a typical routine.

"Hi, Mike. Can I get you anything to eat?"

We leaned in to give each other a quick kiss.

"Na, I'll just rest a minute. How were the kids today?"

Robin says that I was always a great dad. I really need to know that. Of course, I made mistakes, but it is very important to me that I was a good dad.

On the long days when I worked late, Robin would catch me up on how the family's day went, and then I would go to bed.

So between the normal days when I got home between 5:30 and 6:30 (which were most of the days) and the occasional late nights where I just caught up with events and fell asleep, most of our time was normal. Nevertheless, there were a few dark days, maybe once a month or once every six weeks. Those days were the defining moments, and they were not pretty. It was as if I would build up internal pressure similar to a volcano, and then something insignificant would set me off. Boom, I would explode. It was always out of proportion to what set me off.

Yet we always seemed to get over my temper tirades, make up and keep moving forward. I would like to say as we built that big house and as we had all that money and were living that lifestyle, that I did not have those blowups. However, the frequency and the intensity never changed. Do you get that?

Money did not fix it. Money did not even really help it. Money was not and is not the answer to our human problems. This is hindsight, for when I was living it, I never bothered to think about it this way. I was still pushing for more money. I was still obsessed with that fear of failure, letting it drive me forward without taking a good look at my situation or my motivations. With so much money, I could never have predicted we would be a month from homeless and me a few months further out from jobless.

During these difficult times, Robin and I established a tradition for our children. We made sure we took a vacation on the beach every year. We made it all about the kids, playing and doing whatever we could to make that week a fun one for them. I believe we missed fewer than five summers of beach fun.

It actually started just before we became parents, when I was away for two weeks training with Nationwide Insurance. We really didn't have extra money at that time, but we were paying our bills and doing okay in our first home. Julie (my mother-in-law) rented a house on the beach in New Jersey and Robin went down, pregnant with our first child. I came down for the weekend and bought Robin all kinds of little gifts and things from Columbus, Ohio, which was the training facility for the company. I wanted to demonstrate I had been thinking of her everyday—she was so happy to see me, and I was so happy to see her. This was just a very nice time. We both enjoyed it so much.

We tried to make this week a priority every summer. We figured that once our kids grew up, the tradition would fade away. I am happy to say I was so wrong. Our kids are grown up now with families of their own, the whole gang of family members now rents out two to three houses, and we all troupe down for a week of fun on the sand. This now includes in-laws of all types and their kids! Instead of losing people as they grow up and get married, we just get more (this was for summer 2012).

We had a huge gathering during the vacation for Lucas' second birthday. Aunts, uncles, cousins—all sides of all families. All the kids were provided with little hard hats to wear, the boys got yellow and the girls pink. There were so many people crammed around the table singing while Lucas played with his cake that I couldn't fit everyone in the lens of the video camera! Oh yes, I'm that one—the one that is always zooming in on the fun at a family party.

I have been filming since the days of VHS tapes, when you had to balance the camera on your shoulder it was so big and probably weighed five pounds. I like to be behind the scenes with the camera and my son Alex does too. At a young age, he would grab that huge video camera, sling it up on his shoulders and make a home movie. There is one where he catches our whole Thanksgiving Day event. Including Mom and Lindsay sticking their tongues at him, Regal, our beagle, and then he gets us all to say, "Hi, Chad" and pans around the room to catch us all—so he can send that to his big brother who is missing the holiday serving in the military overseas in Iraq. AJ also narrates as he films, having fun with it all, but also taking it seriously.

One camera moment that really made me feel connected to my son and my family happed while he was in high school. At the end of one filming session where he is filming his friends at a drum core practice, he says something that just catches my heart.

"Hurrah for being young!"

Hurrah indeed. I'm so proud of my kids.

So AJ gets the camera bug trait naturally. I must have every year filmed and saved. Most of the adults just roll their eyes at me and move out of camera range. However, the kids usually ham it up when they know they are on camera, and I catch all of that. It really warms my heart to be in a mass of giggling kids of all ages—brothers, sisters and cousins—all packed into the rental houses like sardines. Controlled chaos. I love it.

Nevertheless, to balance this all out, there was the dark side of my life in the eighties and nineties.

* * *

Imagine that you wake up each day, and when you get out of bed, you put your feet down on the ground and walk around starting your day. Oh, is that what you do?

Now imagine that you wake up each day, get out of bed, and gently lower your feet on the eggshells, which cover the floor. You walk as lightly and carefully as you can in order not to crush the shells; it takes vast amounts of concentration. If I would tread too hard, I would crush the shells and fall through to the snarling hell that I saw in my mother's raging face. This is what I felt my whole life until sometime in the late eighties. Although I had bright spots in my life and a wonderful family, I was still living with PTSD. It sneaks back once in a great while now. Just living with that feeling of uncertainly, the exhaustion of always being on high alert, it affected every aspect of my life, just as my anger did.

I am going to share a few stories to illustrate how my life was infused with anger boiling deep inside me. Anger is an intimidating, illogical emotion, and most of the time, anger originates from the effects of fear and pain. Anger is a method of self-preservation; sort of the mind's way of saying the best defense is a good offense. Whenever I see a person consumed by anger now, I know they are in deep pain. I don't look for insult in their angry words but try to offer up my own story and help them get a peek at that pain to realize they can find a better way through life. They can find a way to happiness. But like so many people I talk to today…

I didn't realize I was angry.

I just thought it was other people and how stupid *they* were being or just me running into dumb bad luck or being flat-out cheated by someone. The point I want to share with you is that anger and pain can lash out in many different forms. Mine was a quick fuse on my temper, arrogance and extreme levels of anger once I went off. I danced right on the line of being in real legal trouble, others were, and are, not so lucky with how they acted out. Extreme anger can lead to extreme behavior and land a fellow in jail. I was right there in booking and slipped through; today, I know it would not have happened like that, and I would have spent time behind bars.

No matter what, it all sifts down to the fact that we are responsible for our own actions, and if we make a mistake, that's okay. However, we do need to face it, admit (perhaps turn ourselves in) and then work to make amends. We need to work tirelessly at not repeating this damaging behavior. Just remember, it's all a learning and growing process. Each of us may act out somewhat differently; it really doesn't matter, the motivation is the same.

These are some of the things I have done that I am not proud to write about. I wish I could take these actions back, but we never can; I never can. It pains me to think of them, but I have to share it to show that we all can change, and we all can get out of that rut and find a happy and peaceful life.

In the early days of operating that video store, my partner (I'll call him Jeff for the sake of his privacy) called me on the phone. He was very excited about the biggest sale we had made so far. He had sold a new VCR and rented out the *Godfather* VHS tapes to the tune of some $700 (back in the early eighties). I was also excited, but something told me this was not all going to go smoothly. I asked him to tell me the address that was printed on the check...sure enough, it was from the worst part of Norristown—there was no way a check for this much was going to be good. I told Jeff this is what I figured, and I took the check directly to the bank in the morning—no good. RG (our deadbeat customer) had written a check out of a closed bank account. I'm not going to share RG's full name, this is not about getting back at him, and I even hope he has done better in his life. That is how I feel now, back then I felt righteously angry and was determined I was going to get my equipment back.

I strapped a 9mm pistol under my suit jacket and gave a .357 Magnum pistol to Tom, one my oldest and most trusted friends and off we went. Tom was a little bit taller than I was; we were both dressed nicely, but we were both determined to carry out some justice. It was like a scene out of the movie *Deathwish*.

We knocked on the door of the apartment listed on the bad check. A cute five-year-old boy opened the door; I asked to speak to his mother. She came right to the door and listened quietly as I gave the name of the person on the check and asked if he was there.

"Oh, that's RG alright, but he's not home now. RG lives upstairs anyway. He don't live with me no more."

"He wrote a bad check for a VCR."

"He already sold it, sorry."

"I'm going up to check anyway."

So Tom guarded the front door while I went upstairs and walked right into a stranger's apartment. There was a VCR—not mine—hooked to the TV. The two *Godfather* tapes were right there on the coffee table. We had store stickers on all our tapes, and I did see them, so I do know for sure they were our tapes. No one was at home. The mother was in the doorway—threatening to call the cops. I could see her turning the large cordless phone over, so she could punch in that 9-1-1 number. (Remember those huge cordless phones?) I could also see the fear and anger in her eyes. I didn't care. I was only concerned with getting my stuff back. No one was going to get one over on me!

"I'm calling the police NOW!"

"Go ahead," I snapped at her, and I just kept walking further in toward the TV and the other VCR.

I figured I would just take my tapes *and* the other VCR. If he wanted this one back, he could return the one he stole from me, and we would exchange. I began unhooking the other VCR from the TV, kneeling down to get at all the wires. I heard someone running up the stairs. A young man (not the one that gave us the bad check) was rushing up, just clearing the top stair and heading right toward the apartment I was in. I swiveled my whole body toward the door in my crouched position. I locked eyes with him and slowly stood up. I opened my jacket and showed him the butt of my 9mm.

"If you come any closer, I'll blow your balls off."

"I'm not moving."

And he didn't. Thank God.

I truly don't know if I would have shot him. I am now brutally honest with myself about my past, and I just don't know which way my action would have fallen if he had decided to come in the room. As it was, I put those bulky VHS tapes on top of the VCR and walked out the door and down the steps.

As I exited the building, the cops pulled up. One of the officers knew me and just wanted me to leave the VCR and tapes on the hood of the car, where I had placed them.

"Mike, you know *we're police officers, and we* can't march into a house like that."

The other cop was demanding our arrest, or he would report his partner to the sergeant. So, they arrested us. We were not even handcuffed, just asked if we had weapons.

"Yes."

Then we turned the guns over and sat in the back of the car. Off to booking, where the "nice" cop was looking at my 9mm trying to find the serial number. I reached forward; he handed me the gun, and we were both leaning forward looking for the serial number! Well, he knew me, and I sure was not going to make some big escape—I had money and lawyers. Still, that is a scary and an amusing scene that would never happen in these new post 9/11 days.

The whole incident turned out fine. We were booked at the Norristown, Pennsylvania police department and released on "our own recognizance" to come before a judge later. I was charged with breaking and entering, trespassing, theft, receiving stolen goods and terroristic threats in addition to lending a firearm to my friend who did not have a license to carry a firearm. This was for stealing from someone and nearly shooting another person—all from my self-righteous anger.

I wonder about how quick I was to anger in situations like this. I could go from being a really good guy to ballistic if I thought I was being taken advantage of. In this situation, could I have been homicidal just to keep from feeling used?

A majority of people who are victims of abuse have suicidal thoughts and feelings of being unworthy. Was I being homicidal, so I could fight off being suicidal?

I think that is possible in hindsight. Whether you turn the anger out or in, extensive damages in many areas of your life will occur. I am sharing it here, so others can take a deep look at the behaviors that seem to sneak up on them. When one has been abused, much care is often used to make sure it doesn't happen again. It can manifest in anger, withdrawal or a myriad of other behaviors that all seem more extreme than a situation calls for or even that do not fit a situation at all.

Race, wealth, intelligence, religion; it doesn't matter. Child abuse happens in all social classes and categories. Unfortunately, approximately 30 percent of abused children end up committing some sort of a violent crime and end up in jail. That is not even counting the ones that are arrested for drugs or prostitution, all stemming from childhood abuse. It, therefore, affects all of us because anyone of us could fall victim to a person acting out in anger, as I have done on many occasions.

Did RG's girlfriend and (I'm assuming) brother deserve to stand there, just feet away from me with a loaded gun and full of fury? No. No, they didn't. It happened anyway because I didn't recognize that I was even angry or in pain. I was so focused on myself and my needs that I didn't even consider that I was terrifying that woman, that I was really threating to kill another person. Don't forget I'm a good guy. Imagine all that pain and anger living inside someone who was not as fascinated and open toward other people. What a mess, huh?

Here is another story of which I am deeply ashamed. Once, in the early years of my marriage, Robin was standing in the doorframe between the kitchen and dining rooms. I have no idea now why I was angry that day—but I reached out and with flat hands gave her a shove with one of my hands on each of her shoulders. I watched in dread as she went flying backward about three feet. She landed on the linoleum floor and kept sliding backward until her back hit the kitchen cabinets. I had just flung her completely across a room! I was shocked at myself, very sad—sorrier than I could say. Of course, I apologized and remained more loving and attentive for months after that. Then I guess it just faded from the front of my mind, and I slipped back into letting my temper take over. I never physically abused her since that time, but I would still rage, intimidate, and verbally beat her down

Another big anger event occurred at my brother's wedding. It was toward the end of the evening, the reception was rolling along under full steam, and everyone was happy and enjoying themselves.

I was drinking much more than usual. I rarely did that; I still don't have much more than a single drink at dinner or in the evening occasionally. I don't remember much about that night; certainly whatever made me angry was so important I have forgotten it *(snark)*.

That tells me my anger was an extreme form of some kind of pain because the issue couldn't have been that important since I have forgotten it. Something touched a painful spot inside of me, and I reacted in anger. Interesting that such a scene was sparked by something so small I can't remember it. But I do remember lifting up the kitchen table so hard it hit the ceiling. Dust and bits of ceiling rained down on me. Other family members took my sons out of there. Robin found her own way home. All the rest is fuzzy, but I woke up in the hallway the next morning with a ripped and bloodied tuxedo.

My anger was escalating because I had not figured what was causing all of this. If I did something stupid out of anger, I would just address that one thing—asking for forgiveness or blaming it on someone else. Talking only about that single, isolated event. I would never get out of the anger trap until I could see it for what it was. I was not enlightened at this time, so my blood pressure kept going up and down.

I was talking to my dad on the phone one day. I got some of the story from an attorney who was renting a room in the back of my insurance office. He overhead me as rage took over.

"I'm coming over to kill you."

Then he heard me calling my brother Stu to come over to the office right NOW.

Stu and I left in a screech of tires. I stormed into my dad's house, banging the door behind me so hard Stu had to wait for the slam before he could follow me or risk having his nose taken off.

I immediately started to choke my dad. Stu was in the doorframe watching. Dad was not fighting back. I was shaking him, watching his eyes. God. I must have looked just like my mother when she did the same thing to me as a boy because she thought I lied to her. God forgive me.

The blinding rage that that household gave to me and my siblings was strong.

As I was on the way to killing my father, Stu was urging me on from the doorway. Telling me to finish it. Maybe we felt like if our parents were dead, we would be set free.

In the end, I must have seen the resignation in his eyes. He wasn't fighting me and didn't fuel my rage. Ann must have taught him well. My murderous impulse died out. I removed my hands from his throat and stomped out.

I growled at him, "You are going to die a lonely old man."

The last incident I am going to share with you is not so volatile, but it shows how I had my wife walking on eggshells around me every day of our lives. That is no way to run a marriage, and I am so ashamed I put my lovely wife in those situations. This particular tale started out on a Sunday morning.

Robin's youngest brother Eric was having his confirmation that day. At that time, Eric was a blonde-haired loving child. He was quite a bit younger than Robin, and we were able to help raise Eric as our kids were all very little at that time; Eric adored them, and Eric was with us more than he was not. We had been married about seven to eight years at this time. I loved Eric. My reactions had nothing to do with it being Eric's confirmation day—it was all a part of the dark cancer inside of me.

Earlier that month, we made plans to go to the church and then go to my mother-in-law Julie's for a confirmation luncheon. Remember that Julie loved putting on a party, and this celebration would be no exception. She always did put out a good spread.

I'll use Robin's words to describe the rest of this scene.

Mike likes his sleep. I'll leave it at that.

So I got the kids up and fed them breakfast. I had two of the three kids in highchairs at that time, I think. Then I put them in the tub to scrub off breakfast. Got them all dressed nice for church. Then I got myself all dressed, and I went to wake up Mike. As great as he was as a father, morning was not Mike's best time.

I would have to chirp, "Mike...Mike...Mike," most times when I would wake him up.

This day, I was thinking to myself that he is already annoyed because he doesn't want to go to this thing. So I am just going to make it as easy as I can on him. I did all the work with the kids and so forth and then went in to wake him up. So far so good...he gets up and heads off to the bathroom.

We only had one bathroom, and my curling iron was still plugged in. I wasn't quiet finished with my hair. That was it. Just that one little thing that was not right was enough of an excuse to set him off.

He started in because it was morning, and he was grouchy. He just wanted to sleep in on a Sunday, simple as that. If it wasn't the curling iron, it would have been some other little thing. He was in one of those moods.

"Jesus Christ, I can't even change in here with this damn curling iron..."

I went into immediate action, running in to grab the iron and get it out of his way.

"Mike, please don't start."

I was trying to keep us moving forward and maybe out of the danger zone, that did work sometimes. But it was too late. It just got into a screaming match.

"I'm not going…"

"Don't do this to me, please…" and I'm now crying.

I kept begging for him to go. Well, he went; the day actually turned out to be okay. But that was it for me. I had walked around on eggshells long enough. I thought, "I'm really done. I'm tired of this happening for no reason."

When we came home that night, I said to Mike, "That was the last affair that I am going to go to with my face all swollen from crying. So you either get some help, or I'm packing these babies up, and I'm out tomorrow."

That was probably only the second time I put my foot down. And I was serious.

The next morning, I called a therapist. I had gotten the name from my brother Marc who was already seeing this therapist and had recommended her. I took the next available time slot; it was just days after the Sunday incident. I knew Robin was serious, as she never threatened to leave or ask for a divorce or take the kids when we had arguments. I could also see it on her face.

I loved Robin. I loved my kids.

I was hoping the therapist would help Robin to get over being so emotional. Since I wasn't going to chance losing Robin by not going, I was also hoping this was not going to be too much of a waste of time.

CHAPTER 10

Therapy? I Don't Need No Stinking Therapy

*Often, teenagers from violent
homes turn to drugs and/or alcohol for
release and comfort. Many escape into early
and poor marriages and/or pregnancies.*

—*Breaking the Cycle, 2002*

That I adore my wife, this is not in question. It shook me to the core to know that if I didn't work on my anger issues, she said she would leave me. I was still looking at events such as how I acted at my brother's wedding as isolated incidents. If things were different at a dinner or event or my bathroom, well then, I would not have gotten angry. Therefore, it really was not my fault. Other people had to be more considerate of me, or so my theory went at that time.

I didn't need any therapy, but I did need Robin. I knew Robin was deadly serious about this, so we set up an appointment with Brenda B. Bary, PhD, a psychologist located in Lower Merion, Pennsylvania.

She is a lovely woman. Average sized with a gentle face and grace in all her movements. Her voice is soft with just the hint of a Southern accent, or perhaps I get that impression because she is like a Steel Magnolia for me, strong at the core, but soft and beautiful. It was pleasant to walk into her office, a professional and nicely decorated reception spot and a cozy room for individual therapy and a larger room for groups. The reception area was bright and well lit, while lamps lighted the individual and group therapy rooms rather than ceiling fluorescent with an awesome view of the Philadelphia skyline. This was perfect. I would be able to let Robin work on her issues with this therapist, while I relaxed and enjoyed the soft voice, nicely decorated office and awesome view.

This may sound like a contradiction, perhaps it is. Although I went to that first therapy session with the singular goal of appeasing Robin and therefore keeping my wife, I did plan to be honest and to have an open mind. Thank God that I valued being honest at the time, so that as I "played the game" of therapy, I was actually able to find out some truths I didn't want to admit and some truths that I had been hiding from myself. I was not an easy character in those early days. Dr. Bary handled me with ease. (Her patients do call her Brenda, but for this book, I want to honor her talents and professionalism.)

Here is how the first session went:

Robin and I went in together. The impression I gave off was of an older brother, driven to succeed and to stay in charge of my marriage, my life and my wife. A person who never had his own needs for love met and was put in a position of caring for and being in charge of his siblings. This left me with a well of unmet needs and an obsessive drive to succeed to keep ahead of any empty spots. It also left me fighting to prove that I was worthy, that I was not useless and weak, that I was not like the image I had of my father. In working so hard to be different from my father; I had taken on some of the domineering aspects that my mother exhibited. I could tend to be a bully with my wife who, due to her own childhood issues, played into this pattern. This, of course, was not shared with me so bluntly that first session. Dr. Bary had my number quickly; I just didn't know it yet. She ended this first session by explaining to us patterns that people often fall in. She used this to teach Robin and me how the past tends to replay in the present. This glimpse into human nature resonated with both of us, we could each see a little of our parents' actions in our own. We still had filters on; we were not ready to see the whole picture yet, but it was a great start.

The funny thing about that first session is, I didn't think I gave off any hints of anything other than a decent husband who was there to support his emotional wife. Funnier thing, I ended up going to therapy solo after about four sessions with Robin.

Our second session together, we worked very hard at trying to see ourselves objectively. No blaming, just looking at how we interacted with each other and with others. Once we had a good grasp of really seeing ourselves, then we worked on how we could see these hidden patterns and work to change them; work to make things the way *we* wanted them to be, not to follow a dark path of knee-jerk reactions. Finally, we were given a homework assignment; we were to write our autobiography.

As Robin and I worked together in our third couple's session, we each took a look at our parents. Now that we were seeing ourselves and seeing patterns, it became clear that Robin was trying desperately not to be like her mom, and I was trying very hard not to become my dad. The ironic thing was, this was setting Robin up for being a peacekeeper in order to keep from being nagging and bitchy. These patterns were setting me up to be more like my domineering mother! I was not being sadistic or inflicting physical harm as she did to my family, but I was being dominating and controlling. What a revelation! In no way did Robin want to be a passive partner in our marriage. She is smart, alert, and strong, yet the pattern was pulling her toward suppressing those traits in order to keep the peace with me, and it played right into my obsession with making money and making sure I had the "perfect" home and life. Okay, I said to myself, we have a lot of work to do to get on the right track and fix this marriage. I was just starting to get it, yet still not taking in much of the blame; somehow, I was still seeing the root of the issues as being other people. I was not assigning much responsibility to myself, and I was not giving myself credit for being in control of my own choices and behavior.

Although the assignment of writing our autobiographies was in our second couple's session, it took at least a month for me to get mine finished. I know now it was because I was trying to be honest but still had no conscious memories of sexual abuse. The bulk of my memories dealt with how domineering and abusive my mother was and how she treated my father. At this time, my recollection was how she hit/kicked him while screaming and throwing furniture. Yes, she hit us too, but nothing too gruesome to recall. The volcano was not yet ready to blow…

In our fourth couples' session (I make this clear as I go on to have solo sessions soon.), Dr. Bary had us do a sort of regression. This was extremely difficult for me. I don't think I could have done it if Robin had not led the way in this one. This involved each of us closing our eyes and imagining the first really bad scene that we could remember from our childhood. Man, I was used to running away from those memories. Now this doc is asking me to run headlong right into them.

So Robin took her turn first. She went back to a very early scene where she was three. Robin's mother tripped over her and blamed Robin for falling. Going back that far to something no three year old should be blamed for opened Robin's eyes. If her mind took her back to that incident, then she had been taking on guilt for other people's actions since she was three! As Robin was growing up, whenever anything would go wrong with her mother, Robin would take the blame. It set Robin up to seek out peace at any expense, which is not healthy. While it allowed her to find a way to live with my temper tantrums, it kept Robin trapped in a role where she didn't shine as brightly as she could have, and she took on the blame for many things in our marriage that she had no responsibility for. Just wish I could do this one over.

Dr. Bary turned her soft, yet intense gaze on me. "Your turn, Mike."

Ah, now it's my turn. I dreaded this. Okay. I am going back to when I was ten. Mom was physically beating Dad, and he was just taking it, not doing anything to stop her. I was feeling extreme frustration and helplessness as I could do nothing but watch. Again feeding into my determination to never be the kind of man my father was. I loved him dearly—it was so difficult for a young boy to understand how you can love someone so much and hate how they behaved and feel so betrayed by them.

By this time, Dr. Bary must have realized there was much more buried than I was letting out, and she arranged to have me come in for solo sessions. I was still very strong in my notion that I had come out of my childhood in good shape, and Robin was the one who needed a little more work. So I was reluctant to go solo, and I let my arrogance really shine through as Dr. Bary and I arranged the schedule. I did it just because I loved Robin, and I knew she would insist I follow the doc's orders.

May as well go, can't hurt, and it will keep Robin happy.

For my first solo session, I was really revving up. I was waxing philosophical about other people, and if they behaved in a certain way, then they wouldn't run afoul of me. I know I was doing this emphatically and with vigorous volume. Because I was engaged in a monologue defending myself when no one had attacked me, Dr.

Bary simply rotated her chair around. My voice faltered as all I had to interact with was the back of her head. Hum. She didn't challenge me. Didn't tell me to lower my voice or answer her questions. She just disengaged with me.

Well.

I can't fight or argue with someone who is not fighting back. I don't remember exactly what happened from there, but she got me to calmly engage in a conversation, to realize the difference between that and the tirade I had been spewing out. I was still convinced all the problems I had were other people's fault, but at least I had calmed it down a notch and was expressing thoughts that usually angered me in a more civilized manner.

As we were able to get back on track, Dr. Bary had me describe my interactions with other kids when I was young and in that very tough school. When my family first moved into this new school district, I had been teased because I was short and small. I am not considered short now, but I must have been a little shorter than the rest back then, skinny and too quiet. I made a great target. I also felt scared, which I hated. Now I can look back on my therapy notes and see that the words empty, humiliated and coward were also brought up at this time, showing me that I took on feelings that I attributed to my father.

I never felt good enough and had fleeting suicidal thoughts around the ages of ten and eleven. To defend against these suicidal impulses, I puffed myself up. Somewhat mentally got bigger, not a bully, but certainly aggressive to any hint of being teased or taken advantage of. I joke now, suicidal to homicidal. Though really it was a quick temper, maybe a little swagger, all to keep others at a distance. I never really had homicidal thoughts except one aimed at my father (when I choked him) and one aimed at my mother (when I stopped the physical abuse). I would try very hard to find ways to avoid fights and places where a fight was likely.

After a few solo sessions, another proverbial rock was smashed across my head. Dr. Bary helped me uncover another pattern in my life. It was startling, and after I really digested it, it helped me immensely. I carried on my pattern of being quiet and then exploding with temper that I had shown in my marriage and other relationships to my business life! I would partner with others who seemed stronger than I did, maybe liked to run the show, and I would work in the background for a certain period of time. Then somewhere down the line I would flip, my temper would burst out, I would dump that partner and take charge again. It was like I would be stuck being Dad in a business relationship for a time until I built up energy and anger at the situation and then I became Mom, ruining that partnership with vicious anger. Sometimes, the business survived and kept making money; sometimes, it caused me to lose big. Certainly, there was no stability in this pattern. I couldn't build a strong business if I kept falling into this pattern.

So after a few solo sessions, I did what is called a weekend intensive marathon. This is where people work on deep issues, so I was able to see other people strangers to me, working on their own painful issues.

At this weekend workshop, there was one woman whose story really hit me; unfortunately, she had been sexually abused by her own father. She was sharing this terrible story with us, sharing without fear. Seeing this, knowing that it wasn't a weakness that led to my being a child victim, I realized that any human who went through such an unthinkable series of abuses would have to have created ways to survive. I started to release myself from some of the responsibility. I started to realize that a six year old could never be held responsible for such acts. I also saw that no one was disgusted with her as she told her story, that everyone seemed to care and was committed to helping her heal. They didn't hate her. Maybe they wouldn't hate *me*. I had felt hated all my life. For the first time in my life, I could actually visualize telling the truth to others and feeling compassion from them.

It was the dynamic of seeing other people sharing, of having a doc that was strong but still soft, of knowing I was in a safe place, and there would not be anger or blame; all this helped prepare me for the real work that was to come. As I came to the realization that a person could be a strong person, have a backbone, yet still be soft and honest and supportive, then I was ready to be that kind of person. It was at this time that I unexpectedly opened Pandora's box, which led to the memories of mother-son sexual abuse.

So began my long journey and hard work under the guidance of Dr. Bary. Make no mistake, if you want to get something out of therapy, it is going to be hard work. My journey was long and included individual, group and weekend intensive sessions. It would start with just a little sharing, with me letting just a little bit of information out. Let it out not just for Dr. Bary, but for my conscious mind also. As each piece did not cause the doc to look at me in horror, I felt a little safer to tunnel down for a little more. For me, it was worth every uncomfortable moment, every tear, every shock, and every emotional breakdown I had. This is because what followed each of those difficult sessions was a relief. It was a weight off my shoulders, which gave me more energy for the rest of my life. It gave me more energy to devote to my family and friends and just enjoying life.

That was years ago when I was really locked into therapy. I had the expectation that when I "finished" therapy, I would be "cured." End of story, and life would be as if I had been normal from birth. Of course, it doesn't work that way. I will take some scars (literally and figuratively) to my death. Still, the lessons I learned and the skills I developed have given me a "happily ever after attitude." Nevertheless, there is no secret way to overcome your issues; I want you the reader to understand this, so you won't be disappointed with how your own therapy sessions are going. Just understand your particular patterns, know you are not alone and know there is always hope and a way to make it better.

Here is something I wrote during a time when fear was trying to take me over. I won't call it a relapse—but it was a few steps backward, and I hope that your seeing my words will let you know this will happen, just ride it out and mentally fight your way back out, it will be worth it.

> Today is a day of struggle! I am trying to balance appropriate and inappropriate thoughts. After spending years in some form of therapy, I still fight these demons on a daily basis. It has gotten easier over the years; however, it still poses problems nonetheless.

I now attend group sessions regularly. I have finally found a support group for men sexually abused as children. I go to share and listen with others who can relate to my extreme experience. It is a great feeling to be there and share with other members the relief, the support and the safeness of unburdening oneself in a group session.

Here is a poignant aside story that occurred as I was in full swing with my group therapy sessions, so I am adding it at the end of this chapter. It is NOT typical of what a person in therapy would encounter or do but is wrapped up in my life story, an attempt at something new, and as my kids like to say, an epic failure.

I had been in group therapy for a while. Unexpectedly, I get a phone call from the host of a popular local TV station. They wanted me to tell my story on their local interest sixty-minute show. The program was *AM Philadelphia* and ran from nine to ten in the morning Monday thru Friday. That show covered all topics in a local news type way—from an honest auto mechanic who also volunteered at the hospital to a kid making nationals in a spelling bee contest to women making a living off home crafts. So the gambit of anything local. Oprah, Sally Jessie Raphael and Ricki Lake were also in full glory during that period.

AM Philadelphia wanted me to talk about mother-son sexual abuse—to break the taboo. I wanted to help take the stigma off this too, but I didn't want this to turn into a drama session or to become some sort of a Jerry Springer shoutathon. If I was going to do this, it had to be respectful, clinical and not sensational. I had never heard this topic discussed publically. I felt that I should speak out about it—bringing awareness and perhaps healing by sharing my story. Then I asked the million-dollar question.

"So, how did you hear about my very personal story?"

Turns out someone (not my therapist) in my group who had no permission to share this confidential information told them. Now, I am not out to put enough information here to identify this person. I knew who it was by the first name instantly. I was shocked that my information as well as my name and phone number were shared, especially by this person. Yet then, as now, I am driven to remove the taboo and to begin talking about this subject so that people can feel more confident about getting involved if they see the signs of this rare type of sexual abuse. Step in, stop it, and get everyone involved professional help. This person must have known I wanted to help others with my story—as there seemed to be no malicious, selfish, or financial intent in what they did. I know I had mentioned in group sessions about wanting to reach out and take the stigma off talking about family sexual abuse. Therefore, I guess the sharing of my information did not come totally out of left field.

Therefore, I set any blame aside and figured this person felt my story was so strong that it needed to be shared with others. Yet I was not ready for cameras or strangers. I telephoned the host Mr. Kennedy and requested that he NEVER call me again.

I talked it over with Robin. I shared the offer and my fear with my group. After about six months, my group had convinced me that I could do it. I decided I could do my segment on the show. I then contacted Mr. Kennedy and arranged for a filming day and the other things that go into getting a show like that ready. Robin was also going to be by my side. We worked it out so that both Robin and I would be shown in silhouette, at the time I think I wanted both my own privacy, and I thought that not seeing me might have a larger impact on the viewers.

Long story short, I took the step too soon. I was not prepared to talk so openly in front of complete strangers and a camera yet. I sat in that chair and gave that poor host yes and no answers. I did very little talking. I know my sister-in-law recorded the show with a VHS tape. I never watched it; I wanted to speak more about it in this book, but I think the tape has been lost to time and moves.

I hope that my bit on *AM Philadelphia* may have helped someone realize they are not alone, that they can overcome and create a new life. However, back then, there were no e-mails or voice mail, no easy way for a viewer to get in touch with me.

I guess the lesson I took away from this experience was that I could share my story straightforwardly now. I see how it does help others. Nevertheless, back then, it was far from easy to talk about it. All our painful stories are hard to shine a light on, but once we embrace the truth, it all gets easier and easier, never a piece of cake, but easier.

I'll never know the aftermath of that show, except that I felt I flubbed it.

Oh well.

CHAPTER 11

Digging Back Out

Child abuse occurs at every socioeconomic level,
across ethnic and cultural lines, within all
religions and at all levels of education.

—childhelp.org/pages/statistics

The vision of Robin on the floor packing boxes when we had no place to take those boxes was forefront in my mind. It was heartbreaking for me.

Robin rarely asked me for anything. As we were making plans on just how we were going to handle the foreclosure or short sale of our dream home, Robin asked me not to consider renting a place. She would rather have a small house that she could call her own. OK. We are about to be homeless, and I have only a month to pull this off. I had a fresh bankruptcy on my credit history. I was determined to network for all I was worth to see what kind of home I could find.

A friend of ours, who was a realtor, found us a little home. It was in the worst condition you could imagine, but she said the house was vacant, and the owners wanted badly to get rid of it—so they were willing to "hold the mortgage," which meant we could pay them, not have to get a bank approved loan, and move in within the week. This was a rent-to-own setup or a lease purchase with the stipulation that we get a mortgage in five years and pay off the current owners. I was not so sure I could get a mortgage in five years, but it was either make that agreement or become homeless with three kids.

We located and moved in to a little house that was built in 1960. It was 1991 when we finally moved in. We are in that same house today! It was really a mess, but at least it was structurally sound. We had to rip off ragged wallpaper and rip up yellowed linoleum, then paint every room. The next project was the kitchen, which had rotting cabinets and a stove with burners that decided when they wanted to work, a bit dangerous. This set the pattern for the next twenty-one years and still counting. One project at a time, one room or thing about every six to eight months and then save some money to start on the next room.

There were times within those first ten years that we were so poor we fell behind a year and a half on our utility bills. At one point, we owed the electric utility PECO nearly $7,500! Nothing moved forward on the house during those times. Food became an issue as well. Feeding our three children was starting to present a problem.

A vehicle from PECO pulled up in front of the house unannounced one day. I walked out front to see what the driver wanted. He told me he was there to disconnect our electricity due to nonpayment. I was desperate and could not think of a way out. Yet I kept my exploding anger in check. Oh, I felt anger. It was even in my voice when I talked to this fellow. However, it was not the over-the-top explosion that usually happened. The only thing I could think of to buy time was to push back about trespassing.

I explained to him that the only way he could turn off my electric would be to enter my property. Since I would not give him permission to do this, it would be trespassing. I suggested that he leave right now.

He countered back: if I did not cooperate, he would call the local police for assistance in disconnecting the power.

I told him to do whatever he had to do. I stood in my puffed up way legs slightly apart, arms crossed. There was no welcoming look on my face.

He went to his truck and spoke on a two-way radio to his office. I listened as he explained the situation to whoever had fielded his call at the office. They told him just to leave the bill with the resident, and they would schedule another date for the cutoff. He did just that! Good man. Whew, another chance, a little breathing room and a little more hope to get us through. Another silent prayer answered.

Robin once said to me, "Mike, we have two eggs left in the refrigerator and six slices of bread. I need your help."

I was a proud man. I wanted to be the best father and husband. I had been wealthy just a few years ago. I cannot describe the panic that was creeping up my frozen toes.

At this time, I was on lithium, having just been diagnosed as having a manic-depressive personality. Those two words. Manic. Depressive. A label can affect almost everything you do for the rest of your life. My medical records will reflect any type of mental disorder till the end of time. For example, if you apply for life insurance, your previous psychological history will be available to every insurance company that verifies your medical history. In my case, a misdiagnosis would haunt me for another four years. My diagnosis was actually depression, simple. Damn, I was just starting to realize all the suppressed memories and the real horror of my early childhood. It is my theory that being under such constant stress as a young child did things to my body. I have some health issues, and a chemical imbalance that the lithium was working on. It did help tone down the bouts of anger in a physical manner while I worked on my mental control through therapy. Although I was a much better man while taking the lithium, I was also in a big fog and not at all productive.

Just taking each day as it came to me, a little fuzzy on details and certainly not alert. When we hit the point of two eggs and some bread, that started to cut through the fog. It shook me up that we were so close to total despair. I had to get out there and do *anything* I could to literally put food on the table.

For about three years prior to this wake up call, I was not able to hold a job. Robin held the whole family together. We squeaked by on the severance pay I received from Nationwide two years earlier, and Robin went back to waitressing. They were really hard times. My skills were not marketable anymore because the insurance business was changing. I couldn't even go to a different insurance company. I still had a decent car. I had traded down around the time of the bankruptcy, but I knew with kids, being mobile was important, so I had come out of the trade with a good solid car, an Oldsmobile Toronado.

At that moment, I was not even able to afford the $6.00 cost of my lithium—a blessing in disguise. After a few weeks without lithium, the fog started to lift, and I asked Robin, "How long have we been living like this?"

"Three years."

Now I needed to get off the lithium. I knew it had helped me chemically; however, it removed any desire I had to achieve or be productive. If we were not on the brink of starvation, I would have stayed on lithium a little longer. I also knew that my therapy work was making a difference in my mental control over my behavior. Still, it was harder to deal with the memories of sexual molestation without the lithium. The medication had helped me to be able to bring some things to my conscious mind without falling apart. I needed to let the memories have their time. I couldn't have done it without the help of the medication as my abuse was so disgusting in a visceral way, so horrible, it could only be explained with lithium. Now I was mentally stronger, I had ways of controlling the feelings of hurt, pain and embarrassment that came with the memories of being in bed with my own mother. I had new ways to look at what happened and to not judge me as I knew myself now, but to evaluate the situation and understand it from the point of view of a boy who not even a teenager yet. So, off the lithium I went.

This was nose to the grindstone time. I had to take any job to get some cash flow in to feed my family.

I swallowed my pride and went out and got a job as a newspaper delivery man. That's right, I went from $150,000 a year to $10.00/hour and a family of four to support. Times were so tight that sometimes we would have only fried egg sandwiches to eat. Any of you who are around teen boys know how much they eat!

Before this, for some reason, I still thought I was too good for any job but the kind I wanted. My life had really been crumbling around me for three years; I was in a drug-induced fog (prescription, but still). I seemed to have been in slow motion for a long time. Yet even in this state, Robin and I made sure that our kids were as insulated as they could be. Even more so, we made sure they had decent birthdays and holidays.

One particular year before my fog lifted, we had no extra money for Christmas presents. I drove into a used car dealership a few weeks before Christmas with that nice Toronado and explained to the salesman that I needed to leave there with $1,000 in cash and a car that ran. I ended up with a dented 1984 Chevy Cavalier. It wasn't pretty, but it did run. The cash was for our children, to give the kids a decent Christmas morning. Well worth it.

Robin made her own sacrifices for Christmas. It was another Christmas, and we always started a gift envelope in August to save every little bit we could, so the kids all had a good holiday. It was just a few days before Christmas, and we were wandering in the mall—all the shopping finished. I think we were just enjoying the glitz and bustle. Anyway, we passed a store that had a Miami Dolphins jacket on display. Chad was fourteen that year, and he just *loved* the Miami Dolphins. This jacket didn't look like one of those cheesy things, it was sharp and well done. No one would be caught dead in one of those now, but back then, it was the hot thing. Robin knew that our son would go *crazy* for that jacket. He was a great kid, they all were. We really wanted to do something over the top for him, that jacket was calling us.

It cost $90 (in 1980s money). Robin decided that she was going to use a diamond earring to pay for that jacket. We went home and got the one earring—Robin had it in a small bowl, waiting to find the other one, so she could wear them again. She said the other one must be lost as it had been months, and since the mate was still not found, it was a sign. Back to the mall, we hocked that earring at the jewelry store. We got that Dolphins jacket. We really had to make things special occasionally, didn't we?

Maybe there are people who may claim, "Well, that's just ridiculous." They may think it was a poor choice on our part. We could have put that money toward bills or something else. However, for us, it was, well, we needed a dash of surprise and specialness occasionally. I don't regret it for one second. We still love Christmas so much. I think it was some of those times that got us through the dark and rocky ones.

We always made sure that Christmas was a time of happiness and warmth with some presents for everyone. We would sit on the floor with the kids and just let all the rest of our troubles fade away. Here is what Robin and I get to orchestrate these days with our adult kids: each family comes to our house on Christmas Eve. They come in the door all loaded with matching boxes—looks like it was out of a magazine. They sit their bounty down by the chair or sofa where they usually sit. As everyone settles in, I can look in the living room and see different stacks of presents…each stack is festive and well-matched—a pile of perfect gift boxes. Yet each stack came from a different house, so each stack has a different pattern or color scheme.

We have an amazing meal. We wander to the living room and look each chair with its own stack of picture-perfect gifts. Then we pass them all out to whoever they are for—and now the patterns and colors are all mixed up. Now the festive chaos is about to really start—visually cued by the magazine perfection, which has morphed into wild colors, sizes and patterns.

Then we DIG IN. Oh, the joy of all of the kids talking at once, filming, putting batteries in new toys, the cries for Poppy to "look at this!"

Lindsay once said to Robin, "I want my kids to have what we had growing up."

That means the world to us as parents because when I look back, I think of so many of the times that weren't so good. I feel guilt that I was depressed, or I wasn't in the here and now for my kids because I had too many worries. But I guess we must have done a fair job of it after all.

* * *

Now I was off the medication, working hard early each morning and then going on any job interview I could in the afternoons. It was maddening because I would often even be called back for a second interview, but I seemed to always come in second place. I knew I had the skills and the drive, but I was always falling short of getting that good job. The early mornings of the paper route were starting to take their toll on me. Still, something in me was pushing; I was determined to work myself out of this rut and save my family. It was a vision in my mind as I drove by myself in the dark each morning. *I will not let my family down.* But this was not the false pride of being on the money treadmill as before; this was a desire to surround my family with stability and peace.

I didn't want a flashy car. I never even thought of a better car now. I wanted a warm and comfortable house and kids that got to be a part of the extracurricular activities in school because I could afford the equipment. I wanted laugher and kisses from my kids and wife. These visions of spiritual happiness (not material possessions) was all that was keeping me going now.

I was driving at 3:00 a.m. one morning, right in the middle of a nasty snowstorm. There was not another soul on the road. It was slippery and dangerous. I was gripping my steering wheel, concentrating on driving and feeling a little sorry for myself. Truth, a lot sorry for myself. Then I was running through the apartment complexes where I delivered the newspapers in waist-deep snow.

Driving on the main road again, I passed a strip mall and one sign—in bright neon—was shining out in the storm. It was that time of morning when the sky was as black as it could be, which I saw out the side and back windows. With the snow pelting down in front of me, it was almost blinding white. It was an eerie contract—perfect darkness and blinding whiteness. The sadness of being in my early forties and delivering papers and risking my life to do it hit me in the glow of that sign and the contrast of white and black.

I said, "God, is this what you have in store for me?" Then I kept on.

I kept on for another few months, and spring was finally arriving. This one nice spring day early in the afternoon, I was delivering the missing parts of papers; if anyone was missing a section or even a whole paper, they would have called in their complaint by the time I was done with my delivery route. This ended my daily routine—taking the missing sections to customers. I had a large canvas bag slung over my shoulder and was walking in the sunshine, feeling fairly good in the warmth and the moment.

"Hey, paper man," the sound of a strident stranger's voice broke into my relaxation. I didn't want to turn. I had a feeling my nice day was about to end.

"Hey, paper guy!"

I had to turn. I saw an old balding man coming at me. He looked disheveled and sad.

"What can I do for you?"

"I'm missing the TV section of my paper." There was a pause while he aimed an angry look at me.

I was frozen. I felt the anger rising up from my toes—it was creeping up around my shoulders. I'm sure my brain was about to send some smart-ass words out of my mouth—thank God I stood there and simmered for a second or two—as that was long enough to let this annoying man start to complain again.

"Do you know what it is like to live alone and not know what is going to be on TV? I always go to bed on Saturday and know what I am going to watch the next day."

I was able to say with no emotion in my voice, "I have the TV section here, here you go." And I held it out to him.

He wasn't finished yet...

"I'm going to have to complain about this. I can't have a missing TV section in my paper. I pay for that paper. I pay for delivery."

I could see that this touched on the only bright spot of this man's day. He was hurting. He was angry, but not really at me. He was hurting because he was lonely, and he felt no one cared for him at all. I could relate to that feeling!

"I'll tell you what, I will make sure that I look in your paper every Saturday to make sure that TV section is included. You take this TV section now, and I'll make sure I do that for you."

His face actually broke out in a grin. "You'll pay attention? You'll check my paper for me?"

"I sure will," I chirped with enthusiasm. I was not faking it—he could tell I was going to make sure he got that TV section.

And off he went. As he left, I felt something open inside my chest. A loud and strong cracking sound, yet there was no actual sound. It was like ripping a dozen arrows out of my chest. It was physical and audible, and yet not any of those things. It was something that helping this annoying man did for *me*, and I knew this was an answer to the question I had asked God only a few months ago. *God, what do you have in store for me?* I then heard two words coming from above; "it's over." What exactly does that mean? There was no one there but me. I came home and told my wife what had happened.

I had to help people who were in pain. I didn't have to be mean to protect myself. I realized it didn't hurt me when I let the man complain and raise his voice as he talked to me. It didn't hurt me at all. When he felt I was really listening to him, that's all it took. But the missing TV section offered to him was not enough. He needed to know that someone else understood he was in pain, and then he could accept that missing section. Then, although nothing on the surface had changed, he felt better—and so did I.

On days when everything went smoothly with my paper route, I had time to head over to what I called the Labor Corner; it was a part of Manpower, and they had day labor jobs for pickup work occasionally. Not long after that TV section incident, I received a phone call from Manpower and was hired with three other guys for $7.00 an hour. That job was building a chain pet store in Montgomeryville, PA. It was going to last a few weeks, so I was very happy with that.

At lunch, I couldn't even go into the local Wawa convenience store and buy a sandwich and drink, that is how broke I was. But I sure wasn't going to let this job slip by me. I was wide awake now and determined to dig out of this mud hole. I did my best, showed up on time, and Robin made me lunches for the rest of the time our little gang of men worked there.

At the end of the building project, they were going to let us go. I was resigned to looking for more work again. The foreman called me over as the other guys were leaving.

"You wanna work another three weeks?"

"I sure would like that," I replied.

"We like how hard you work, and we'll need help hanging the ceiling tiles."

Excellent. A small reward for hanging in there and always giving my best. Another three weeks would really help with the bills. It was closing in on four to five years of struggling, jobs on and off with nothing steady and none of the jobs being fulfilling or for good pay. We were paying just enough on the utilities to keep them on. Our mortgage fell behind. We were told we would have to sell this house if we didn't catch up right away.

The year was 1999, and I had just filed bankruptcy for the second time in eight years. I was one year behind on the mortgage payments, and I filed the second bankruptcy to delay the mortgage foreclosure. I owed everybody and their brother. Our attorney suggested that we sell our house and try renting. He stated that no one will lend you money when you are as deeply in debt as I was, did not have a full-time job and in bankruptcy. I remember Robin's words clearly to this day, "I'm not losing another home."

She was angry with me and starting to really feel down about her life. I didn't blame her. I was able to comfort her, showing her I was working out of the fog and did have some good things to point to. Still, we were facing losing this little home we had now worked on so hard.

I asked my accountant for a referral, and he suggested a savings and loan. He gave me the name of his contact at the bank, a Mr. L.M. (full name withheld) who at the time was vice president. I made an appointment to meet this gentleman a few days later. As I was driving to the meeting, I wondered how I was going to explain to this man everything that had occurred. Where do you start? What do you say? How could I let him know that it wasn't me being lazy, but being in a fog for years. That I was out of the fog. Who would want to know that? What banker would even care?

Well, I decided to be brutally honest and share my story from the beginning. After we shook hands and exchanged salutations, I was escorted into his office and took a seat in front of his desk. L.M. is about 6'7" and fairly thin, so he was not as imposing as his height might suggest. He gave me a warm smile and asked how he could help me. I asked him for fifteen minutes of his time to explain; he smiled and nodded at me to continue. I explained, boy did I explain.

As I began to get into the physical and sexual abuse, L.M. lowered his gaze to the top of the desk. I wasn't sure why he was no longer looking directly at me, but I was too afraid to ask. Too much depended on getting this loan.

Suddenly, I saw tears begin to run down his face and onto the desk. Terror and confusion ran through my head as I was not sure what to do. I just kept telling my story. After a few minutes, he looked up at me and asked me how much I needed to borrow. I didn't understand his question and said, "Excuse me?"

He asked again how much money I needed to borrow. This time, I replied $160,000.

He looked at me and said, "I think we can help you."

He said it would take about two weeks to process the paperwork. I thanked him for his time and left. I drove home and told Robin what had just happened. I told her L.M. didn't ask for a full name or social security number; for that matter, I never completed a loan application. He just told me we would have a settlement in two weeks. I was afraid that after they checked my credit, they would change their minds.

Well, we settled in two weeks, and I am happy to report I have never made a late payment since then. This event clearly could not occur today. There is just no way any lending institution would approve money to anyone who is in bankruptcy and a year in arrears on their mortgage. It is my personal belief that I had divine intervention. I leave it to you, the reader, to decide. Had L.M. been abused himself? Had he known someone who was abused? Perhaps he was simply full of human connection, and he knew I was sincere and at a place where I could make a new start of it. I don't know, but it changed my life; that simple additional chance to get back on track. Thank you, L.M.

My credit has recovered significantly since those days, and I no longer fear the bank or credit man. Let me go one step further to be perfectly clear, my credit is excellent and allows me the freedom to choose with whom I will do business and the rate I will pay. Now that's hope!

Robin was still waitressing, a very hard job, and I was promoted into management at the paper! That gave me steady hours and a decent bump in pay. With our youngest in first grade, Robin was able to pick up a few more shifts—we started to climb back out of our hole. Scratch our way out. Believe me, we owed *everybody* money. Friends, family members: $500 here and $1,000 there.

Little by little, we started to pay things back. I would pay my friend just $50 at a time, that kind of thing—we had kept a list of who lent us money; but it was horrible. It was a horrible, horrible time in our lives. I would almost break down when I looked at the list of people we owed money to.

We would take the kids to their T-ball games, and Robin would wear sunglasses to hide that she had been crying. She just wouldn't want to talk to anybody. She would tell me, "I just want to go home and put these kids to bed and go to sleep."

Sleep. Such a mixed blessing. It was a way to escape from the anxiety. But used too much it could lead into depression and another rut. We had to stay out of that rut! No matter what. I think we both had what I would call walking depression.

The pressure, the stress was just so bad, and it had gone on year after year. Literally, one of the kids would say, "I have a trip. I need $5.00 for school for Friday."

Robin would say, "Oh, Mike, it's every day, where are we going to get $5.00?"

We emptied every change holder/piggy bank/jar/couch cushion—Robin remembers getting in her car and driving somewhere and screaming to herself with frustration. Even cursing at God, "What did we do? Every job interview that Mike gets, something goes wrong. It's one let down after another. I can't take it anymore."

I think on some of my job interviews they found out that we had a bankruptcy (back then they were not as common as now), and that made them not want to take a chance on hiring me. We were down, and everything was linked together with the bad credit history. Desperate. That's the word. We just felt so desperate all the time. And I watched as Robin continued to spiral deeper in depression and wanting to run, hide and sleep.

All the while we were trying to keep the depth of this reality from other people. We were really living as subhuman in some ways. In the summer of 1994, it got to be the worse; I remember my Robin saying, "Mike, you know I grocery shop on the weekends. That is tomorrow, and I have no money. This is all the food we have."

She was making fried eggs and toast for dinner. I told her, "It will be fine. It will be fine. Something will break, something will break."

The expression on Robin's face said it all, *Ha, yeah, it might be my foot up your ass.*

After holding the manager's position for a year and Robin's extra shifts at waitressing, after paying back some of what we owed, we felt a little breathing space. We felt we were going to make it! Somehow, we managed to never be crazy at the same time. I look back at that and think that is how we got through it.

Robin once said about me, "And God love him, he was a cheerleader." But she was a cheerleader too. Seemed like when one of us really hit bottom, the other one was able to shoulder the burdens, tell the other, "It is going to be okay," and keep slogging forward.

Robin has been a very loyal wife—she stayed with me, worked with me and helped keep the whole family on track during this difficult time. I've been sharing all the hard parts of my life in this book, but I hope you have also seen the good times. The great holidays. The love. The fun birthdays. The beach vacation most years. And just the fun we had as a family every day. We always had love for each other, and we always found ways to have fun. Now that the weighty stress of owing money has been lifted, it makes it better, but we never lost the joy of living.

In the midst of digging out, I created the business I currently have. I am a public adjuster, property insurance adjuster who assists the insured in their property claim. We work for the homeowner, NOT the insurance company. The insurance adjuster will come out to look over any damage or loss and then try to negotiate for the lowest amount the insurance company thinks it can get away with paying. As a public adjuster, I am in the other corner, negotiating for my clients and making sure the insurance companies pay them a decent and fair settlement for their claim.

It is fun for me because I really know the business, having been an insurance broker for many years; I know all the little games that are played, and I can stop them cold. We can haggle, discuss and toss things back and forth. One thing I know is my clients will never have to settle for a low-ball offer from their insurance company. That is another little kick for me personally, as even my job now is helping people.

My business has been steady for many years. I still love going to work in the morning.

CHAPTER 12

The Unbroken Cycle OR Forgiveness

*30% of abused and neglected
children will later abuse their own children,
continuing the horrible cycle of abuse*

—http://www.childwelfare.gov/pubs/
factsheets/long_term_consequences.cfm

My youngest brother, Stu, fell into the money trap as hard as I did. His wife, Lisa, was raised very comfortably and the privileges growing up with wealth brings. She is a lovely person, both outside and inside. After many years of marriage, both Stu and Lisa have grown to realize the importance of antidepressants; from my perspective, it has changed their lives and relationship in ways that, at one time, were inconceivable. They now grow each day, and I am so happy to watch it happen! May God continue to bless them and their family.

Stu has been married for over thirty years, and they have three children, two boys and a girl. Stu and I have grown close over the years. He happens to work in the insurance industry in Pennsylvania, and our offices are only a few miles apart. We speak almost daily in some way, whether it is a phone call or a quick visit during a break in the day.

I have no memories of Stuart being sexually abused, but Stu says he went through the same torture that the rest of us did. I left home the second I could join the Air Force, and Stu had been around nine at the time. I think this is why I only have memories of Stu being yelled at and beaten with the rest of us, but not of any molestation.

Stu also harbored bitterness and anger, just like I did. He took a different form. Everyone's take is different as we are all unique and will react differently. Stuart has always been something of a poet, writing little things for special occasions. Some funny, some beautiful.

Stu is really making me proud these days. Once his repressed memories started to surface, he had a rough time (like I did). My breakthrough triggered his own memories when I started to share with the family what I was working on in therapy. A while ago, Stu started to take antidepressants. It helped him deal with the memories without becoming overwhelmed. As he was working through this and decided that the money trap was a hoax, and he needed to con-centrate on his family, love, joy and peace over material possessions and constant anger over the past.

This decision threw some waves into his marriage. In order to face the discussions and make the best long-term decisions, Stu stopped taking the meds to make sure he had a clear head…once he made those decisions, he went back on the meds and has been on them since. He is literally transformed! He is growing every day by leaps and bounds. I love spending time with him and listening to him as he shares his new ideas and new outlook on life. Lisa, his wife, has also grown significantly, and we really enjoy spending time together.

My transformation took longer; well, it is still a work in progress.

* * *

One never knows what path is going to be put in front of them. Here is a set of circumstances that put me on a collision course with my parents.

My mother had a job at an elementary school; she was a *"child aid."* After I had been in group therapy for a while, my group suggested it was partially my responsibility to report her past behavior to the proper authorities at the school. The question that kept playing over and over in my head was what I knew, how could I permit my mother to be around children?

I was too scared to do that. Maybe eight months to a year later, I finally did it. I went to the school, and I met with the vice principal because the principal was out, and I started to tell him my story. As I proceeded to explain my history, the vice principal became very uncomfortable and asked me to stop! He didn't want to hear my story; he said he had lost a son to suicide because of this very issue. I didn't understand his thinking. I still don't. Did he mean his son was abused and committed suicide, yet he didn't want to work to get an abuser out of the school? Or what? He was emotional and very remorseful; I didn't have a good opportunity to follow up.

That blew me away—I just left the school, and I didn't want to deal with it. I went back to my group and told them I'm not going back; it's not my responsibility anymore. I'm not responsible for my mother.

They said you're responsible for the *children.* So I ended up having to go to the superintendent of the school district. I sat down with him and started to tell him the story, and he looked at me and said, "Why should I believe you? Your mother has an exemplary record."

It was the very first time since my recollection of facts that anyone had questioned my memories. It took me aback for a few seconds. I told him he could check with my brothers and sister to corroborate my information. Marc didn't want to be a part of it; but

Michelle and Stuart did, and they spoke with the superintendent. She was terminated.

My father called me that night and said, "Your mother was fired today, and we are thinking of suing you for defamation, libel and slander."

My response was immediate. I said, "Maybe that would be a good thing, Dad."

"What do you mean?" he replied.

I followed up with, "Because then, everything would be public in a court of law, and everybody would know."

That was the end of that. It died a natural death, and she never worked again.

As I was working through my issues in therapy, I wasn't all sweet and loving to my father either. I remember there was a period in my life when we didn't speak for over five years. I wrote him a three-page letter twenty years ago that I never sent. This letter is full of raw feelings; maybe I should have sent it to my dad, maybe not. I am going to include it at the back of this book so that any reader who wants to share some raw feelings can feel my example.

We *MUST be able to* identify exactly what is having an effect on our life in order to understand, grieve and let it go. That's what this letter did for me. I worked through it all, gave it all a name and didn't hide my feelings. I thoroughly enjoy my dad's company each week these days.

So I wasn't a little angel just because I started therapy. But as I became more aware of what happens when a child is abused, as I realized that the abusers were once abused, my eyes and ears were more open, and I was catching hints about my mother's past from her family members. I pieced together some basics of her story throughout the years.

My mother's parents were from Kiev, Ukraine. My grandfather was a tailor. Since I have no recollection of him because he died before I was born, my only information on him is from my mother, and I know she was looking back through her own special filter. Still, I have talked to her sisters and brothers occasionally, and I think I have a clear, if brief, picture now.

According to Ann, her father, Isadore Epstein, was a good-for-nothing useless alcoholic. She said it was her "job" every night to go to the local bar and drag him home.

Her family settled in Reading, Pennsylvania. My mother is one of seven children: five boys and two girls. The ironic, sad, and typical behavior is that both my mother and her sister were sexually abused by two brothers. As I understand it, they lived in poverty for many years. Perhaps this is part of the foundation of why she pushed and blamed my father for not having earned more money.

My mother shared a shameful and resentful admission about her relationship to her father with me one day. "The only thing I wanted from him when he died was that ring on his finger. If I could have, I would have pulled his finger off with the ring." She admits to me with anger in her voice that it was a sick way to feel, a shameful thing to be a focus at his funeral. I think it was a feeling that he owed her something, and she was damn well going to do anything to make sure she got some of what she was owed.

My mother shared little snippets over the last two years of her life after we were reconciled. Like her family history, piecing it together, I had a fuller picture of what may have driven her to the edge of insanity. My mother did want to get married and have a family. She was looking at it as a way out of her bad life. While they were never as poor as her family had been, my father never made it big. She had been banking on marriage, making everything financially better for her, especially no more money worries.

She resented that this did not happen. My mother also expected that she was going to instantly have the love and affection she never had as a child—that this love would be given in great amounts from her new husband and children. Her expectations were pure fantasy—there was no work required from her; nothing *she* had to do to ensure this.

I got the impression that since my father was away working so much, my mother looked to me, her oldest child, for counsel or empathy. I didn't have any for her.

The bitterness that must have swelled in her heart when she still had to struggle with finances, when she needed more love from my father but never asked for it or let him know about her feelings, how horrible that must have been. Her expectations were that it all came automatically. I can only imagine the despair she felt after realizing (incorrectly) that her life was now a hopeless mess with no love.

This must have been the main trigger for all the verbal and physical abuse. Lashing out at her family because she was so unhappy. I don't think it makes sense as the trigger for sexual abuse. No one other than her sister would talk to me about the sexual abuse they endured. I have never been able to get a clear, concise understanding on how that happened, how it stopped and how it played a part in how she decided to sexually molest her own children.

If only she could have expressed her unhappiness and shared how awful her childhood had been—to us, to dad, to a therapist. Maybe she would have had the opportunity to grow beyond her dysfunctional roots and maybe, just maybe, life would have been different for so many people. Wow. What a tragedy.

* * *

Even with my therapy on solid ground now and settling into a stable but not obsessed relationship with my income, I would wake up every morning with my stomach feeling like a washrag being squeezed dry. Just like wringing water out of a washcloth, my stomach was that knotted up each day. I was still doing battle with my past but desperately needed to move on. I still suffered from PTSD and had a host of physical problems which I think stems from the stress hormones that must have been coursing through my little body when I should have been focusing on growing up strong.

I take statins for cholesterol—my body keeps working up a tolerance, the docs keep increasing the dosage until it is almost dangerous, and then I start on a new generation of statin and do it all over again. Unfortunately, I also take medication for blood pressure, a beta blocker for my heart, Effexor for depression and six others for various heart issues. It is my personal and professional belief that the level of stress endured over a prolonged period of time directly inhibited my ability to develop and grow in a "natural" manner (without the stress hormones). I'm experienced at not feeling well emotionally and just noting it and doing whatever I can, yet getting on with my day (some people call this *survival*).

* * *

One morning, I woke up and felt strange. I couldn't put my finger on what was "different." My mind and body were giving me strange new sensations. I worked through the morning, still feeling strange. Not pain, just strange. Then as suddenly as a lightning bolt, it hit me while I was relaxing my brain at lunch.

I didn't hate my mother anymore.

Just like that!

I realized the physical sensation I had been having was a NORMAL stomach. No twisting or knots. And that this was because I didn't feel hatred for my mother anymore. Oh well, the realization came to me in a snap; but it took over forty years of life and fourteen years of intensive therapy. It took living with anger and tension for over thirty years, being an ass to many good people and even a bully at many times when my anger really took over. So it was a long time coming. In addition, I never had forgiving her as a goal. Her actions were *not* forgivable. My mind must have been working on this quietly in the background for years. It came to my conscious mind in the blink of an eye. Weird.

So I picked up the phone and called her, "Mom, can I come over and see you?"

"Yes, I'm home right now."

"Okay. I'll be right over."

I had seen her multiple times each year; it was not as if I had shut my mother and father out of my life. They did seem to be adoring of their grandchildren. Of course, I never left my kids there alone. I had set up in my mind that Robin or I would always be there if our kids were there. And the abuse, the yelling, the horror of our childhood was never discussed. However, things had always been stiff and formal. I also never touched my mother in any way—I had a very big personal bubble when I dealt with her. So my call to her that morning was not totally out of left field, yet she had no idea of my state of mind.

I pulled up in front of her house. I looked at the white metal-framed screened door and sighed. I remember this moment like it was a movie.

Shutting the car door with a heavy *thump*.

Walking straight up to the door. By this time, she had heard my car or my car door and was standing in the doorframe.

She opened the screen door, standing on the inside and holding the screen open with her left hand/arm and kind of smashed back against the wall to let me in. Normally, I would have walked right past her and into the house. No touching. This day I walked forward, looking her right in the eyes and held my arms shoulder width apart and straight out to her.

The classic human "we are going to hug pose."

She let the screen door go, and it eased closed on my back. She curled her right hand behind my neck to pull me into her, and then she rested her head on my shoulder and started to cry.

"I'm so sorry." She sobbed into my shoulder. "I'm so sorry." Sniffling. "I'm so sorry, Michael, so sorry."

Another "just like that." That is all it took as far as communicating the importance of what was going on right then, but we both knew I had finally found a way to forgive her. She had never asked for forgiveness. I had never set out to give it to her.

It was really too hard to talk about. We cried a little, had some iced tea and just talked about the safest subject—my kids. I made it a short visit. It was very emotional for both of us. Neither she nor my dad were really able to go back to those dark days and face them. So as a family, we just ignored them, as we had been doing forever. We were able to now have a relatively "acceptable" mother-son relationship.

A typical day with my mom AF (after forgiveness as I call it) was quite pleasurable. I would call her and ask her out to lunch once a week or so. She usually said yes. I would pick her up, give her a hug on the porch and open the car door for her. We had nice, general conversations at lunch. Then I would drive her home, give her a hug good-bye and go about my business for the rest of the day. After each of these lunches, I really felt good inside and honestly enjoyed the visit. I would call her two or three times a week for a quick talk.

It is not all *like happy days*, there were times at lunch when she would talk about something that made her angry. She would physically start to display that rage I remembered so well—these signs I was very, very well acquainted with. Yet, now I knew from naming my own inner anger some of what must be boiling around inside of her. Because I understood her rage now, I didn't have to feel defensive about it.

When she would start ramping up into anger, my response was to express sadness that she was getting angry and being sorry for about whatever she was talking about having hurt her enough to anger her. I would ask her if it was possible for her to forgive whatever it was she was talking about. Many times, she would think about it and mellow out. What a different outcome our lives may have had if she could have received the proper help. I keep talking about this book just reaching one person and helping overcome their trauma, just one person who doesn't pass on the cycle of hurt, anger and violence. It will have a ripple effect and cause a waterfall of lives to be better!

This relationship lasted for two years, and then she died suddenly. Of course, there were still stiff and awkward times even after that day of forgiveness, like I mentioned might happen over lunch, but I had fully forgiven her for the unforgiveable—I even know she went to heaven.

Weeks after her funeral, while standing on the porch at my dad's house (the same porch where we had that emotional hug), I saw her spirit in the front yard. She was looking at me, and then she just went up toward heaven. I knew that meant that somehow she had made it to heaven. Perhaps she did her own repenting and praying in those same decades that I was taking to work out my own issues. I know she loved me in her own way. Those last years she even started calling me a pet name, Michaela (sounds like Mike-a-la).

Funerals can be tricky for us humans. While I went through the day saddened that my mother had died, I knew I could not sing praises about her when I stood up to give my eulogy. As it turned out, I was not the only one with mixed emotions in attendance. My brother Stu was in rare form that morning and requested time to share his eulogy, but that's another story I'll get back to soon.

Robin had a totally different experience at the funeral. It seems the wives and girlfriends were not treated like family—they were seated in the back of the funeral home. I was so wrapped up in feelings and what was going on that I didn't notice this.

So Robin was back there with the kids and neighbors. She had certainly paid enough dues with both me and what I put her through as well as my parents who were not welcoming to her when she joined the family. Also, my mother was never nice to her. Ann would bark out orders during visits, was short and always pushy toward Robin. Not a joy to be around. Perhaps it was because Robin and the girl-friends were not Jewish that the rest of the day's events happened as they did.

There was only one Jewish funeral home in the area, and looking back, it seemed they must have had a tight schedule, crude as that is to think about. They were eager to get us all out to the cars and off to the gravesite. My father, brothers and sister were ushered into the limousine—and Robin says that car went flying down the road to the cemetery. The girls were trying to follow and were losing us. They finally broke out in giggles because it was all so surreal and crazy.

After the graveside services, we went back to my dad's house. Robin had loaned out her tablecloth and other items, so the house was set up properly for entertaining family and friends. Robin had put in a lot of behind-the-scenes effort to make the day run smoothly. I was still clueless, moving around and talking to people. Robin was getting angrier at me and the other men because we were clueless that we were shutting out the women. We were so engrossed in our own conversations. Robin was feeling the weight of years of misuse by my mother, and now it was all being capped off by being ignored like a "good little woman" who was staying in the background.

One of my aunts noticed Robin's slow burn and took her outside for a walk. Just a little bit of sympathy had Robin crying. When my aunt acknowledged that they all had seen how nasty Ann was to Robin for so long, that there had been no reason for it; when Robin heard it out loud from another person, it was so cathartic it allowed her to forgive what she needed to forgive. She felt acknowledged as part of the family—despite the whole day being set up around anger and sadness.

Sometimes, people mistake Robin's helpfulness and tendency not to argue as a weakness. I know how strong she is, how brave and powerful it is to offer kindness to people when they are hard and nasty toward you. Robin is a hero! We should all remember that even heroes need acknowledgement and a thank you now and then. I am pleased to say that Robin forgave my tunnel vision from that day.

I have forgiven the unforgiveable. Unfortunately (from my point of view), my siblings were not (are not) at a point in their lives where they could forgive her. They had a stormy relationship with her until her death. I believe they still hate that lady. Who am I to judge? I just wish they could find real peace—I hope their stomachs unknot, and they feel some relief someday.

Marc was closer in age to me than Stu, and I think because of that, I felt closer to him for a long time. Marc has been married and divorced twice and has a fourteen-year-old daughter. We live only four miles apart; he owns a retail auto title/tag/insurance agency in Pennsylvania.

Marc has been in and out of counseling for many years, attending a twelve-step program when necessary. Marc has been working on the physical and verbal abuse we suffered as children. He is working through the childhood trauma, and I am very proud of him. Marc and I have spoken, and he knows about my memories of sexual abuse and that I clearly remember him being similarly abused. As of now, he has no memories of this, it will happen in its own time. It is hard, and it feels shameful, like it is your fault—of course, the fault is never on a young child—but I can tell you it sure feels that way when you start picking through the memories. Not only that, but the pain and terror and confusion seem to be just as strong when you bring those memories out—like it just happened!

Because of this dynamic, we have not been very close for the last twelve years. I still talk to him once in a while but haven't seen him in almost a year. I don't want to push; I know how hard this is. So I try to let him know how proud I am of him and continue to pray for his healing and recovery.

Stu may be working toward that relief now. At the time of our mother's funeral services, he made it clear he was not at the forgiveness stage yet. I knew I wasn't going to get up in front of people and talk about what a wonderful person Ann was, but she was my mother, and I had forgiven her, so what was I going to do? I gave a short speech; something along the lines of "you never wanted to linger, you got your wish." Short and as sweet as could be given the circumstances.

When Stu got up to speak, passing me as we switched spots, he growled, "I don't know why any of you are crying. She was not a nice person."

Then he proceeded to read a ten-minute poem going over all the horrible things she had done to him. It was not graphic; after all, it was poetry, so it was cleverly guised. At the time, I felt this was a bitter act, but from Stu's perspective, it must have been a coping mechanism and maybe felt like something that needed to be said publicly. Looking back and many years later, I now believe this was his way of coping with a horrible situation the best way he could.

Ann's sister-in-law reacted to my brother's poem with a statement along the lines of, "He must have needed to get that off his chest." Ann's side of the family were all gathered in a group. Nothing more was said. That was all they could muster to say about his poetic eulogy. To me, this was simply another example of my family not wanting to face reality, not wanting to deal with the truth and face the hard facts.

I was thinking that they didn't seem shocked at what they heard! I felt they must have suspected this all along. But what was their solution? I get that they did not want to have the difficult conversations and may not have known how best to address their concerns. But what did they expect would happen? As a result, at least three generations in one family were forced to suffer the consequences of silence. Three generations *at least*.

I want every reader of this book to take away one thing if nothing else; if you see abuse of any kind going on, speak up! If it is not a situation you can or should put yourself into the middle of, then report it to the police and let them investigate. No one wants to be abused. No one deserves to be abused. It *IS* our problem because these victims carry around vast amounts of anger that presents at various times and affects our entire society. This can't be taboo any longer. We all have to take responsibility and get involved.

My father still is not able to fully comprehend the ripple effect of his actions or lack thereof. When I told him I was going to write this book, his only strong reaction was that he didn't want my mother to be shown in a bad light! She's been gone for fourteen years. He still prefers to keep his head in the sand. It must seem safer there for him. I've accepted the relationship for what it is rather than what I would like it to be.

I have learned that it is normal for someone who was abused to feel extreme anger at both parents when they have their own children. That is when we realize just how innocent, small and fragile children are. Then they have that strong feeling of protectiveness toward their own children and wonder why their parents didn't provide that for them.

The cycle needs to be broken. Kids deserve to grow up in a safe, caring, loving and supportive environment. I wonder how anyone could hurt a child, but people can and do. It is our responsibility to help those individuals overcome their anger and whatever other issues they have for the sake of creating a safer environment for future generations.

CHAPTER 13

Are You Ready for Some Football?

One in three adolescents in the U.S. is a victim of physical, sexual, emotional or verbal abuse from a dating partner, a figure that far exceeds rates of other types of youth violence.

—loveisrespect.org/is-this-abuse/ dating-violence-statistics

You may recall I opened this book with an open letter to the victims of Jerry Sandusky. Part of my interest in this particular case is that football has played an important role in my life and development as a person. My very first thought was, "Oh no, a coach what could be worse?" There are multiple male victims, and the abuse continued over a substantial period of time. I felt as if I was revictimized following this story. I could actually feel the pain again.

Fortunately, I'm lucky enough to be a football commissioner for our league, Bux-Mont Football which is associated with Pop Warner. What that means in practical terms is that I am a child psychologist, working with the parents and children, attempting to exemplify appropriate behavior. For me, being calm and speaking softly, taking a little extra time to let a parent or coach express their frustration; this all works best to get us to a solution. Every decision that is made has the child's interest first and foremost. Safety, learning and fun are the most important elements in a successful program.

After coaching sports for more than thirty years, I prefer this job at this time in my life to any other sporting position I have held. Besides that, next year, my grandson will be old enough to play flag football! Imagine the possibilities!

It doesn't have to be football. We all need a connection.

One of the best ways is to volunteer your time at something. It also doesn't have to be an established charity or soup kitchen-type place, although those are great places. What I am saying is that each of us needs to think about what you enjoy and what type of person you either enjoy being around or want to help. You don't have to uproot your life to do this either. Just one hour a week will make a difference to someone else and a surprising difference in your life. So choose or try a few out. Then seek out a way to give back to society. Firefighters to dog walkers to meals on wheels, there is a spot just waiting for your sincere help.

But as you will find out, my connection is football.

Robin understands why I spend every Friday, Saturday and Sunday from September until Thanksgiving on the fields. I love it, and the kids love it. We have one of the biggest leagues on the East Coast with over seven thousand children involved, and you can just imagine the number of adults who participate. The parents and coaches, referees and family members all seem to really enjoy it too. But I never lose sight that I am there for the kids.

I have received some great feedback; I have been honored with "volunteer of the year" award a few times for my work as football commissioner. I just put a lot of time in, and they...they like me! (Once in a blue moon, I will flashback to the feelings I had when I was a teen, when I felt most people did not like me, and that there was nothing about me that was worthy of liking.) Sometimes, the warm feeling that comes over me when I feel I am really a part of this surprises me.

They know that I get it, and they like to have me there as an advocate for the children. I don't blow up or raise my voice. When I could be forceful as the commissioner and start to throw people out, I quietly move everyone toward a solution. I try to handle it in a very diplomatic and discreet way, and I usually don't even report it to the league. Instead, I handle the situation to the best of my abilities. Nearly every time it is worked out, and even if everyone doesn't get exactly what they want, they are satisfied with the solution and work with it.

The really bad, sensational stuff happens only once in a great while, and other than those times, I can calm the situation down. I gesture easily with my hands, slow and circular movements usually low in the field of vision. That usually gets their attention, and then I move toward their space with a soft voice. The soft voice is the key for me. I encourage coaches to let the game play, to forget about the problem and let the game shine. I don't force my way in; there are too many other fish to fry. All I do is diffuse the situation, set things back on track and let the game play.

The kids are not living and breathing football to win. Oh, they love it when they do win! But after the game is over, they want to have pizza and soda, to talk about the excitement of the game and hang out with their friends. It is a game to them, and they're the ones that look at it the best way.

There are a few incidents each year. Usually, new parents each time who haven't learned our league's rules.

Some of the worst are parents who don't realize the danger and push to send their kids back in the game after their child was injured in a previous play. I think they get so caught up in trying to win that they lose focus on what is most important. There was one game in particular, where a player took a really hard hit. The young man came off the field and was taking off his pads. His parent called him over and said something to him—I didn't hear anything. But I can guess what the basics were because when the player went back to the bench, he was putting his pads back on.

So I went over to this player and said, "That was some hit you just took. It would be just fine if you sat out the rest of this game. You can play next game." Then I squeezed his shoulder and walked off. No need to make an issue of it. Let the kid decide after he sits out a play or two. But I also wanted him to know that another *adult* thought he did just fine, and he would still have my respect if he was hurt and could not go back in the game.

I've had parents and/or coaches actually remove the pads that are there to protect their children, so they could make weight prior to the game. So they would cut out or pull out the pads and hope I wouldn't see it when I weighed the teams in. Pull out a tail pad or a thigh pad and hope I wouldn't see it at weigh-ins. They would try to hide it by having the young man pull his jersey out of his pants and keep it loose. So I check them for the safety of the child and do not permit any athlete to play with missing or altered equipment. I just want to make a difference. I hope I do.

When anything like this happens, I don't yell and scream and play a "gotcha" card. If I did that, they would immediately get defensive. They would put up their walls, and nothing would really get done. I get my point across and don't make them feel like demons for trying to sneak one in under my nose. Because I don't attack them, just calmly cite the rules and say sorry this is not acceptable behavior; it is amazing how well it works. Unfortunately, some coaches, just like everyone else, come from dysfunctional backgrounds and need positive mentoring. I hope and pray I can mentor these grownups in a positive way, enough to make a difference.

All this and I get the best seat in the house, which is anywhere I want. Ha! I work my tail off to keep things fair. Do I miss things? Of course. But I keep my eyes open for all I can find, and here is where my hypervigilance helps me again. Not too much gets past me.

I can't help myself; I also look for signs of physical and sexual abuse. Don't think it hasn't crossed my mind that we have cheerleaders out there. I know that on any given night, at least one of those cheerleaders has or will be sexually abused. I can't forget that. That's the torch that keeps me going.

I don't overreact, but if I see signs of something, I'm going to mention it to the school counselor or someone who can then probe a little more; find out what may be wrong with the child. Not jumping to conclusions, but seeing when something isn't right and getting them some help and a safe adult to talk to.

In our society, it seems there is one last taboo. Our society often talks openly about any type of sexual behavior. But the taboo is parent to child: father/daughter, mother/son or whatever combination with the parent. The family is sometimes NOT a safe place, and we don't seem to want to talk about it or set about working on solutions and ways to intervene. We are still uncomfortable talking about it, and therefore, we can't get to the action part where we could, as a society, step in and work on preventing it.

The immediate family seems something we shouldn't interfere with. We can even almost make excuses for a relative, a grabby uncle. But think about it, what adult would put their hands in a sexual way on a child? So what else did they do? How much further will they go if they have the opportunity? I have no idea; I don't know them. But it's there; it goes on, and we are going to tell that story that nobody wants to talk about. And I personally believe that the stories will be told. I believe we (as a society) can make this change. I believe it is going to help many people.

Just think of the violent crimes that will not take place when children have a safe childhood. Just think of the children, grandchildren and great-grandchildren who will grow up happy and pass that on to all the following generations. It starts with us. We have to say it is there, we see it, we want it stopped.

I put myself out there as a bridge for anyone who is angry, hurt or ashamed and thinking they will never get to a different "normal" in their lives. Football is my official indulgence, but it puts me in the path of many people who need support in some form. So does my job as a public adjuster.

Here is where I get another huge kick out of my life. I am a bridge. I find that repeatedly I run into a person who is at the end of their rope. Maybe they hit their wife for the first time, maybe the anger is taking over in other ways. Maybe it is despair, and they are sinking further into depression. Doesn't matter. I take some time, have some coffee or whatever and tell them my story. As they see the pain in my face, the tears well up in my eyes; they know they are listening to my raw truth. Then they get to see how great my life is now.

Almost all of them ask me how I did it. How did I go from such extreme abuse to being an outgoing, happy man with a good job, great wife and a loving family? I tell them "hard work." I suggest they start with therapy. When a professional teaches you how to deal with life on life's terms, you don't feel alone anymore, it is very empowering. When you know it has been done before, you can feel a little more energy tingling in your toes; you just might be able to work out of it too. Then each little victory can give you even more energy.

I don't push. Some people I speak with are not ready to face the truth of what happened or is happening to them. That's alright. Now they know a way, and when they are ready, they can work on it. Some have come back to me after months or years to hear my story again and work on a game plan. I don't judge them. We take life for what it is and figure out how to work on it as we grow. Who am I to judge?

Because I don't judge, I've been able to have conversations with people who are racked with guilt over some crime that they committed. We talk it out; sometimes, they tell me exactly what they did, sometimes not. I don't push. I take only what they are ready to share. I have talked about owning up to our actions, no matter what our motives were. We have to go back and make things better if we can, make up for anything bad that we caused to happen or any sadness that we made people feel—if we can.

One of my biggest dreams was/is of opening an office in a very small town. I see it as maybe half mile square with a few strip shopping centers, flat and open with a mix of some expensive homes dotted about in an older farming community. I wanted to put a sign on the building that read, "Stop in, maybe I can help." I always wanted to be a counselor, and most specifically, I wanted to work with people that did not have health insurance. Why? Because I wasn't planning on charging anything! Here is my reasoning: Do people without health insurance have problems? Right, they sure do. So why would we as a society want to preclude them from our system when they so desperately need some emotional help? We know from all the statistics that if they are *not* helped, they either pass on the abuse to the next generation or become violent and end up in jail—or both! It would help all of us to make sure those who can't afford it get any help they need.

So that is my little secret dream. It's interesting because being a bridge, I do all that without the cute little office and sign. I say I have a traveling sign, and that is my car. Since I earn my income as a public adjuster by educating the insurance company to pay each property claim fairly…in a funny way the insurance industry and their greed is subsidizing my "bridge therapy." I figure that if they knew my fees were going toward helping people, that would absolutely destroy them. Robin always jokes about that: "They keep sending the checks, don't they?" Ha! Oh yeah. Life is good.

I don't have a typical business mind-set. My goal is not to make a profit now. I just don't think about that anymore—I'm off that rat race for good. The great thing is that not only am I happy, but the financial things seems to be working themselves out on their own—all without me being driven on the hamster wheel. Don't get me wrong, I go to work every weekday and often make visits to look over damage on the weekends. I work, and I put in my time, but my mind-set is not just seeing money; but seeing how I can help the people who are my clients.

My friends actually refer people to me! This is the arena that I will stay in until I can practice psychology as a clinician. I am back in school working on my degree. I will further address my current situation later in this book. For my "real" job, I help people with first party property insurance claims. For my passion, I help people who are emotionally lost. I will not turn anybody away who is reaching out, and they seem to keep coming. Someone I have helped may tell another person, "Man, you need to talk to Mike. He'll understand, and I bet he can point you in the right direction."

A bridge. I'm a bridge to the next step in people's lives. Recently, my son (I am not going to name names, so no one will know which son or which friend) encouraged a friend of his to call me. This man, I will call Jeff, had come back from Iraq. It is hard to write these words, as both my sons did tours in those dangerous areas of Iraq. When they were serving there, it felt like I was living underwater. I am so thankful they both made it home again. Back to Jeff and the story.

Jeff had a wife and children. He was a rookie in a police department, coming up for review and seemed on track for being a solid police officer. But Jeff was falling apart. He would sit in his squad car and just watch the world go past. It was as if he was watching a film. He did not feel connected to anything, did not feel passion for anything, and he was letting things a cop should notice pass by because he just could not move. It was getting worse, and Jeff's family was starting to suffer.

Jeff sent me a text. It was like a sting scene in a movie. We met at a diner and talked. Mostly he needed to hear all the bad things that happened to me. He needed to hear about my bad behavior, my repression of the memories. Then he needed to hear how good my life was now. I did most of the talking that night. My son was right; Jeff was just not in the here and now. Jeff said that when he goes to work, the world is just "white noise" to him. He just drives around in the car. He does not stop anybody, nothing.

We met one more time; he talked just a little bit about his own life and more again about me and mine. I told him about my therapist, how it opened my eyes and that allowed me to work on things. It was hard work, but worth every second of it. I told him he was stuck between the devil and the deep blue sea. I slowly emphasized that he had children and a wife.

Jeff contacted my former therapist for an appointment. I believe they clicked, and it was very helpful to Jeff and his family. I suggest that if you are seeing a therapist and are not feeling safe, open, trusting, then move on, just keep looking until you find a therapist that clicks with you. Do not use this as an excuse to be lazy in therapy. Do not go therapist hopping just because you don't want to hear what they say or don't want to do the work and hope to have some magic cure-all session. Nevertheless, if talking to a certain therapist triggers any hypervigilant feelings or is uncomfortable, then search out another one.

Jeff would text me for moral support occasionally after he started his process. I have saved every text. I read them occasionally; it gives me a kick of energy, and I can run for hours on the good feelings I get from that. Jeff is doing fine now. He got it together; he is back in contact with this world and does not feel like he is outside of it.

By the way, I never take any money for this. I do this to make a difference. To help people. Did I help Jeff? Sure hope so. Did I help his wife and kids? I certainly think I did, but who knows what may have happened…from the sadness of a divorce to the tragedy of violence—but something was in the making, and Jeff stopped it cold by reaching out for help.

That's what I do now, and it is because I think most people are good people. The bad are what we hear about, but if most people were bad people, we would live in a constant state of anarchy. People would come in every night and steal your belongings. But they're not! Most people, obviously, are pretty good people. And I do believe that, I do believe that. Yet I think they need help at times (I sure did). And if you bump into me along the road and I'm able to help you, that's cool. I'm going to die with that spark of love for people that I discovered when I was in the Air Force. For me, it's the most pleasurable thing in my life, and it feels so good. I've been told by many people that it is good to help other people, but I *know* it is. So I don't care if others are wrong, right or indifferent, about the value of offering a helping hand. I know it's right. Some people also think I am fake or have some hidden agenda when I help. They can't believe that things are just…well, just good. I don't share many of the dark thoughts; I don't share my pain unless it is to tell my story to someone who may need to hear it. But someone may need to hear the "dark side," not just the wonderful things that are happening in my life now.

Sometimes, things just hit me. It may sound like once I got on the right track it was up, up and away. Not so at the moment, as I am working on this book, fear has me trapped. Trapped to where I don't know…I just don't know what is going to come of sharing this book. I knew writing this manuscript that I would have to revisit some painful memories, that there would be some repercussions. Fear has risen its ugly head now. I want to just run and hide. I want to put this manuscript away and pretend I am normal. I want to sweep all this under the rug. I feel paralyzed. I am fighting the fear now; I can't see it, but I know it's there. Fortunately, I know what I have to do. I can't act like an ostrich, like my dad and many family members apparently did. I have to break the silence and break the taboo.

It took me a week to work out of this fear-based inaction and resume my story. No, it is not at all easy. The fear had me so bad it was almost a full-blown panic. That was a grueling week. The fear caused me to pull away from people and insulate myself from the world. Thanks to my therapy, I'm aware of what this is. The world is my joy. The fear traps me, so I can't get to the joy.

Today, I was tearing up, choking up a little bit. I know what I say seems to some people to be really sappy, and they think I may be telling a lie in order to get my point across. I know what I say to people sometimes makes a difference. I wish I could help everybody, but I can't. However, it is sure nice to help some people. Okay, I am crying in gratitude now. I am so grateful I can do this. I thank God that I can help some people understand there is hope. There is hope. I keep coming back to the hope; it is the spark that can push you to fight for creating a good life for yourself. It is just a great feeling. It must be a reward from God that I can have such positive effects on people. Maybe, it is God's gift to balance out my childhood. I feel every time I help someone, there is some cathartic experience for me. I can bond in some small way with another human, even if it is only through a look or a few words. It makes me feel alive!

It all goes back to that connection, if you don't have one, that's okay, you can reach out and find it. My big one is football. Through my volunteer work, I connect with so many people. In addition, those people refer other people to me. It snowballs. You have to be the one to reach out to connect, other people cannot read your mind, nor are they magic like my mother was hoping for. To be part of their lives, you have to ask for it and look at your own behavior. Once you start to "get it," you will really thrive in the eyes of other people.

I run constantly from the time I wake (usually not before 9:00 AM) until I settle in the house for the night. I'm on numerous medications for atherosclerosis and high cholesterol; I don't eat much during the day, and I am constantly working or talking to people or watching my grandkids. How do I keep going? God has seen fit to let me draw strength from helping people.

I asked God one day if I was a selfish person. I had been thinking about how much pleasure I get from being a contact person for so many in need. I do often talk to God. It seems to me that though I have never heard God answer me in words, but rather I get my answers within a day, week or soon after through events that occur. Not always what I hope for, but some kind of solid resolution. So for this question, the answer was no. No, I am not a selfish person for feeling pleasure when I help people. I am certain of this because right after I was having these thoughts and asking God, I had an experience with a family that was in need. I was able to help the son, and that led immediately to the father reconciling with his son. This situation helped that father and son; it helped me. I can assume it helped other members in that family. Where is there anything negative in that?

I think my demeanor is a gift from God. If I moved to any place in this country, I guarantee you, I would know every dysfunctional family within ten miles, and they would all be calling me pretty regularly. This is because they believe that whatever they need to talk to about, whatever it is, is fine with me. No judgment.

I say, "How can I help you?"

You want to talk about pain? You want to talk about mistrust? Love? Parents? Abuse? Despair? Betrayal? I've hit them all.

I can't describe how energized and recharged and happy I am when I do anything from helping pick up spilt groceries with a stranger to getting a person on the edge into therapy. It all charges me up! The more I give, the more my batteries recharge.

CHAPTER 14

Grey's Anatomy Doesn't Hold a Candle to This

When a child is abused, emotional and psychological trauma can result. A long-term study by the CDC found that, "As many as 80 percent of young adults who had been abused met the diagnostic criteria for at least one psychiatric disorder at age 21." These disorders include anxiety, depression, eating disorders and suicide attempts. Child abuse victims may also suffer from learning, attention and memory problems. Post-Traumatic Stress Disorder (PTSD) is another common problem for child abuse survivors, resulting in constant frightening memories and thoughts, feeling emotionally detached or numb and sleep problems.

—Symptoms of Adult Survivors of Child Abuse | eHow.com

I had a new revelation that just played out over the weekend. It was life-threatening and life-changing and was so startling to me that I believe it requires its own chapter. This event deals with the collateral damage I have caused my children, damage done in the beginning of my marriage when they were very young. I did not even have a clue. Did I repress it too, or was I innocently blind, or did I lie to myself? I don't know yet.

About two months ago, I developed a bad case of diverticulitis. I suffered through the first week of it but could not eat or drink. I finally had to see my family doctor and was put on antibiotics for the second week of this bout. I started to vomit and lost about nine pounds during the last few days. I didn't start out with much extra weight, so this weight loss really weakened me. That sent me to the emergency room of Abington Hospital to be promptly admitted due to the severity of the diverticulitis and my exhausted physical state.

The doctors wanted to do a CT scan, but my bun/creatinine level was elevated (1.87). Creatinine is an amino acid that is connected to our energy level and helps produce protein. Our kidneys create this amino acid for us as well as being found in meats that we eat. High levels of creatinine can cause kidney and liver damage. The symptoms are stomach pain, nausea, muscle cramps and diarrhea. I had all the symptoms. So I agreed to the CT scan.

The emergency room doctor explained that there were two kinds of contrast dyes that could be used for the CT scan; one is oral, and the other is IV (intravenous). Robin, I and the doctor decided that because my creatinine level was elevated (they assumed a dysfunction of my kidneys), they could not give me the IV contrast dye as it would need to be metabolized by my kidneys and may further damage them. So I drank the oral contrast dye and prepared for the CT scan.

After I was in the machine, the medical technician said, "This is going to feel warm and burn a little."

I remembered from my previous CT scan that what felt "warm and burned" was the IV solution I was given that contained the contrast dye. This tech was about to give me an IV dose of dye! I felt a little twinge of fear that something was going wrong here.

"Hold on a second, what are you doing?"

"I'm giving you the IV contrast dye."

"No! Stop. I'm not supposed to get the powerful contrast."

"This is the only contrast we use," she said as she made motions to continue.

"NO! You need to stop right now and check on this; this could damage my kidneys. Go check with the doctor that sent me over for the scan."

She started to treat me as just a grumpy patient. I was insistent. She finally decided to do the right thing and go check. When she came back, she said that I was right and did not administer the IV contrast. After my CT scan, they wheeled me back to a waiting area, and the nurse attending me said she was sorry the doctor forgot to change the order. How do you forget something that might kill someone?

It was an unsettling experience. Sick as I was, I lost my focus and felt a little of my old anger creeping back. I held my tongue, though, and started the admittance procedure. I continued to monitor my temper as I waited eight hours for a room.

The next day, my blood was drawn, and my creatinine level had doubled (3.87), and a nephrologist (kidney doctor) was called. My kidneys were failing, and I was severely dehydrated. The nursing care was inadequate at best. I should have been attended to better and had a saline IV started immediately to fight my dehydration. After four incidents of poor care, I transformed into that scared ten-year-old child I will always carry inside of me, afraid with nowhere to turn and no power to protect myself. After all, I was in a place where they were supposed to care for you and help you heal. I was physically weak; I was now mentally tired. If I wasn't going to get proper care here, then I had to do something to protect myself.

I called the nursing coordinator from my room phone and said I wanted to see her ASAP. She showed up in about three minutes, and I let her have it with both barrels. I told her I was scared of the medical care thus far provided, and I didn't trust them anymore. I was not very nice about it, nor was I quiet. I wasn't yelling, but normally, I speak with a soft voice, a voice that many people have to lean in to fully hear me. I do this on purpose, as it is a great way to not escalate any disagreement—not yelling and de-escalating the situation, as people must quiet down in order to hear what you are saying. Not that day—I was a step from yelling, angry and not giving the nursing supervisor a chance to explain or offer solutions.

Robin hadn't seen this side of me in a long time.

"Mike, relax. Just relax." Robin was trying to mitigate the situation.

I continued on, enraged and trying to intimidate the nursing supervisor. At that point, I had lost sight of the best way to handle this and was just going off. I knew better; I knew how to handle difficult and even scary situations. Something about this had brought me back to being a scared little boy that struck out at people as a form of defense.

Robin made another attempt to reel me back in and tried to make a comment, and I snapped at her and told her to shut up. That did not sit well with my wife. I had gotten away with this brutish behavior early on in our marriage, but this was not how I had dealt with her in years. That shut Robin down, and she wasn't going to take it. She left the room and left me to my temper tantrum.

"You know what, buddy? I'm going home. I'm exhausted too. I've still been going to work and running here to see you. I'm not going to be treated like this. I'm leaving."

Now I was really alone.

After realizing what had happened, I just wanted to go home. My regular doctors knew what happened with the hospital mistake regarding the IV contrast for the CT scan, and I was advised that the incident had to be reported to the hospital medical board. I realized they were taking the incident seriously. If I was given that IV contrast dye with the 3.87 creatinine level, it spelled only two things ... dialysis (kidney transfer list) or death!

God, I dodged another bullet. And believe it or not, all my decisions were made with two injections of morphine. Although, everyone is affected differently by prescription drugs, for me they just seem to have little effect when I descend into the nether world of fear. I become and stay vigilant!

I was calmer now and gave my report to the supervisor. I needed to shut up, relax and let my body recover so that I could go home. That is all I wanted. Just get home and regroup. I was discharged on a Sunday under the conditions that my levels continue to decrease. I was to flush my kidneys by drinking tons of water, and in two days, I had reduced my creatinine level to 1.75.

I still needed to get it under 1.0. So I'll have to continue to flush my system for maybe another week. But I would need to keep this weakness of my kidneys in mind for the rest of my life and keep up with my fluid intake and watch my diet.

Now I'm warm and vertical. I take this as a lesson in mindfulness. It is important to pay attention to your treatment, the reasons for it, and who is carrying out the treatment. In many instances, you will be the best judge of what is right for you.

When I transformed into a scared, angry boy that Saturday night in my hospital room, Robin picked it up as a trigger. She told me she was not scared of me, and she left the hospital and went home. I was so wrapped up in my own temper that instead of realizing how I was affecting her, I just felt a little angrier that she left me.

Just like a two year old would see the world. So I pouted and didn't call her that night. She didn't call me either!

Good for her. The old Robin would probably have tried to make peace, would have suffered through my temper. But my new Robin was not going to watch me behaving badly to the nursing staff. She sure wasn't going to take me behaving badly toward her. I'm proud of her for shutting me down and not allowing me to channel my frustration onto her.

The next day as I was driving home from the hospital, Chad called me.

"Hi, Dad. How are you doing?"

I glossed right over how I was and told him I was pissed at Mom for not standing behind me. Chad had already spoken with Robin about my emotional state and how I had snapped at her and the nurses. He told me this and then went on; he said that when he was little, he remembers that when I was in this place of fear, pain and/or despair, I wanted my family to feel the same thing that I was feeling.

I'm paraphrasing what Chad said here, "When you used to get mad, Dad, everyone around you had to suffer."

Wow. Really? I don't recall ever having that need. Did I? Did I try to take my family down a painful road with me? Did I? Isn't that what my mother did? Oh god!

I asked him to repeat those words, which he did and filled in a little more of his point of view for me. My stomach felt like a twisted washrag. I thanked him for sharing with me. I had to think this all over. Here was a whole new dimension to my behavior, one I had never explored. Truthfully, since I knew how very much I loved and adored my children, it had never, never occurred to me that I had unconsciously done anything to frighten or hurt them. I didn't want to believe this; it is much easier to dig into how other people have hurt *you*. But I had to, I had to face the whole truth of my life and my behavior.

I had always prided myself on insisting that when Robin and I argued over money, we do it when the kids were asleep or outside or gone. I guess that like many parents, I thought I had soundproof rooms. I thought I did almost every parenting thing right, and we only had money problems. Now I realize that the kids were aware of my arguments with Robin and had to suffer the confusion of knowing something was wrong. Also the fear of hearing their father angry and seeing him be intimidating to their mother and probably wondering when Dad was going to turn that power on them. I gave my kids their own emotional baggage! I hung up with my son in a very sad but enlightened emotional state.

I knew I was always loving with my kids. They were never afraid of getting in trouble at school or of bringing home a bad grade and having Dad go crazy. It was never like that. But they had been picking up on the times when I was angry with my wife. They were picking up on the unstable emotions I had been unleashing in the house. Back then, it could have been any little thing, such as my wife letting the fuel in her car run down to empty. Something of no consequence today; back then, it could have been fine, or I could have been building up steam and needing to rage. Very similar to what children of alcoholics deal with.

I then spoke with my daughter who bravely told me that she was scared of me at different times in her life. She went on to remind me of an episode in which I pushed her for running over the garden hose when she was about twelve. She must have been mowing with the lawn tractor, whatever it was; she punctured some small holes in the garden hose. There we were with no money to replace the hose, and I blew up at her. I felt a double punch to the stomach as I listened to her.

So there it was, my lesson. I need to address the collateral damage that I have done to my children and ask for their forgiveness. We never talked about this elephant in the corner of the room. I suppose that my work in therapy and my new outlook on life made them feel that they didn't need to address how I had treated them early on. I do remember that the kids were brought in to therapy a few times, and they would say something like, "Yeah, our childhood was pretty good" and never spoke about the damage I had inflicted on them. I am very sorry for any emotional injuries that I have caused my children!

So…where am I now?

After this epiphany and after having addressed it with my children, am I back in the passing lane? Do these extremes ever end?

I felt like I took a trip on Mr. Toad's wild ride. I guess no matter how sure we are that we have life locked down and we "get it," there is always a curve ball waiting to hit us broadside. Our only defense is to be open-minded and seek the truth in all situations while keeping our tempers in check long enough to let the truth shine through.

CHAPTER 15

A Perfect Summer Day

People are often unreasonable and self-centered.
Forgive them anyway.
If you are kind, people may accuse you of
ulterior motives. Be kind anyway.
If you are honest, people may cheat you.
Be honest anyway.
If you find happiness, people may be jealous.
Be happy anyway.
The good you do today may be forgotten
tomorrow. Do good anyway.
Give the world the best you have and it may
never be enough. Give your best anyway.
For you see, in the end, it is between you and
God. It was never between you
and them anyway.

—Mother Teresa

For each new morning with its light, For rest and
shelter of the night, For health and food, for love and
friends, For everything Thy goodness sends.

—*Ralph Waldo Emerson*

My story comes full circle now. My grandkids are the oxygen I breathe. Here I am, fifty-eight years old and living a dream. I am very happily married, have three successful children with loving spouses and six beautiful grandchildren. My family is thriving, and it is another day in paradise! Who wouldn't want to be in my shoes? I'm laughing now. I bet not one of you would have wanted to live my life now that you know the whole story. But I have to say I am ending my story as one of the happiest, most contented men on earth.

Full circle is really how I feel. Everything is going right side up. My oldest friend was out of my life for seventeen years. We had a service station business together. Then he remarried, and as a result, our relationship ended. The last day was ugly, as he had our towing service snatch the vehicle I was driving. Yes, that's exactly what happened. I woke up, and the car was gone. Since it was titled in the name of our business, I didn't fight to get it back. I signed the papers giving him and his wife all rights to the building and business and just walked away; he still has the business today. Boy I was sure hot at him back then. He was probably hot at me for not being there for him when the business needed both of us. He was married for fifteen years and fought through difficult issues that unfortunately ended in divorce. He's back to being single, and he called me up after seventeen years! In the last few months, we've been getting together and trying to figure out how to make up for seventeen years. Then we realized we don't have to! What an empowering way to look at it. We've got each other, we were fast friends for so long, we know each other so well. My oldest friend is back! I've just got everything!

He said to me, "You're different."

I answered, "I hope it's good." Then we laughed at each other.

Robin tells me a similar thing—in her words:

For just as miserable as life was in the late eighties and nineties; it has been just the opposite for more than the last ten years. And I thank God every day for it because I know what it is like to wake up with that empty stomach, not knowing if you were going to hear bad news. Afraid to go to the mailbox, afraid the sheriff would come to the door at the big house, living through all that fear and not having anything to look forward to but doom and gloom.

Life has really turned around, and Mike is not really even the same person as he was back then. Still a little edge may come out of him, like in that hospital scene, but he is just a different person now. We must have always loved each other along the line because we always fought through everything. We always made it work somehow. Now we get to take a vacation each year and little side trips throughout the year. Financially, things are good, home life is good.

Our marriage is good; we enjoy each other's company—we just got tickets for a show next Friday night. We love the grand babies to death. Mike is obsessed with them (in a great way). It just goes to show that you have to stick with it; marriage isn't easy. Sometimes, I see these young couples, and I think, "My god, you're divorcing? You've been married three years! You can't give it the ol' college try?" I remember we could go a couple of days without speaking to each other if need be. Let something go for a couple of days to cool down and then keep working on things.

There have been a few different people who have said to Mike, "I can't believe Robin has stayed with you through all the financial problems." But we were never crazy together. When I felt like I couldn't take another step and couldn't go on, he would say, "Look, I have a check coming in on Friday. It's going to be fine. We are going to make it out of this. We are going to do this or that. (He would have something inspirational to put in place of this or that!) And then someday when he would be upset about something, I lifted his spirits. As angry as I got at him during those few times when he would rage or bully, he really did keep me from going off the deep end. He always seemed to have a fix for something.

My daughter said about a month ago that her neighbors were over, they were baking or something one night together, and she said, "Mom, we just had a laugh over you and Dad. I told my friend my mom and dad are just so happy. And I can't believe it because they weren't always that happy when they were younger. My dad's still trying to chase my mom, and she's still playing hard to get."

And I thought, "God, I never thought one of my kids would say something like that to me. How sweet."

Isn't that great? See? I do have it all now.

Here are little windows into some of my days as they are now.

A visit where I go to my son or daughter's house to visit or babysit the grandkids: When I first see the grandkids, they come running for hugs and kisses. They smile, and I tell them how much I love them. We wrestle, play house and ride trucks over pretend mountains. The youngest one, John, is eighteen months and just the most innocent child I have ever seen. No agendas—just eat, play and sleep—like life should be at this age. When it is warm, we play baseball, ride tractors, cut the grass and play Barbie outside with my granddaughter.

At some point in the visit, my mind wanders, and I think, "How could anyone hurt these children?" So loving them is a bitter-sweet emotion.

Recently, Lindsay and Scott had to be away from the house for most of a Thursday. Robin went over to watch the kids, and I drove over to join them later, the temperature was in the nineties, so I decided to stop and purchased a blow-up pool. I arrived around 4:00, and they were all so excited. We tried to blow the pool up with a bicycle pump, not much luck. Finally found a spare pump to blow it up, and we all had a ball. My granddaughter who is two and a half decided she didn't want to wear any clothes for the rest of the afternoon. In her little opinion, it was too hot. She just ran around naked— in the pool, out of the pool—all with carefree abandon.

I couldn't help but think, "God, that's the way it is supposed to be." No worries about covering up your private parts, no worries about being yelled at while you are in the middle of a romping good time. All adult things waiting their turn until the right age. Just no worries in the world because Mom, Dad and grandparents will be there to protect you.

The last little window into my paradise, it was Christmas Eve, and the whole family is moving slowly after a grand feast that Robin prepared. I pick up the camera; I can't help myself. I see my little grandson toddling around waiting for all of us to settle down in the living room. I say (from behind the camera), "I love you!"

He looks right at me and says, "I llaalla laaa," which *clearly* is, "I love you." Then he shoves his fists in his mouth as he toddles closer to me. Reagle, our dog, barks and runs in an excited circle on the floor. AJ runs over and takes over the camera work. I guess he can't help it either.

I move forward, "Give Poppy a kiss."

He smiles and plants a sloppy wet kiss on my cheek. No hesitation, no fear. Total confidence in the adults in the room. I take the camera back, and all the kiddos plop down and dig into their presents. Just like years ago with only my three kids—now I have six grandkids, three kids, three spouses, my dad and in-laws…

"Whoa!" comes from the floor as a present is opened. Ryan has opened a remote-controlled airplane.

"Wow you gotta plane!"

Scott is patting around on his chair. "What do you need, Scott?"

"Double A batteries." Scott has a remote control in his hand. And on and on the day goes, the young fathers now taking an active part in this Christmas.

I stand back with the camera and soak it all in. I can watch as the torch is passed to Chad, Lindsay, AJ and their great partners. It appears we passed on the best values we have and true love to the next generation. They are going to be blessed with these, and I see them carrying on the important traditions that help them, in turn, pass on good values to their kids. Those connections make them strong and happy in their own right. I am the wealthiest man on this earth.

I wish I could give out a secret to a perfect life. But there is no secret because there is no perfect life. We are all affected in some way or the other by our family and history. Are there things I regret? Maybe. But it was just the journey. That's all this has been, a journey. And I don't regret the journey. I would never be where I'm at without the journey.

Some people have asked me how I felt when I gambled on real estate and lost our personal wealth. My mind goes to how I feel now. I needed that to happen as it was all part of my journey. The real judgment is how you treated others while going through those hard times. Do you cry every day to everyone you see? Cry so much that they just don't feel sorry for you anymore? Are the people around you tired of hearing the sadness? Or do you say nothing and keep it all bottled up inside (boiling)? There are so many choices in how to handle the bad things that come at us. Now we all can figure out what the hell the healthy choice is—it is a delicate balance like all of life. You share some of your grief with your close friends, family that you trust, maybe a therapist, maybe a support group. Sharing with others is a great way to heal. We are social creatures. Sharing relieves the burden of our grief. Yet that sharing can be the hardest thing to do and the most pleasurable after you do it. The balance is in knowing when you have shared enough for the time being. To back off and mentally process things, to do your own work on your own behavior in your own time. To be aware of the other people in your life and back off sharing your burdens with them when it is starting to affect them in a negative manner. That means you have to understand them and care about them as much as yourself.

I'll tell you the most miraculous and bravest thing I've seen lately. There was this twenty-two-year-old man who came to a men's group therapy session (male survivors of childhood sexual abuse) not long ago. He had been ready to kill himself. At twenty-two! He spoke only a short while and very quietly at that group session. Oh god, did I feel his pain. It makes me grit my teeth right now to even think about that pain. Seeing that feeling in not only my eyes, but in the eyes of others in the group helped him to understand he was not alone. It gave him the strength to get through one more week and come back to the next meeting. How brave to come back? This guy reached out and opened the door to the basement of his life.

I believe both personally and professionally; trauma changes the brain chemistry. It seems the most important factors are the age at which it began and the type, which can vary greatly. These factors, in my humble opinion, directly determine the amount and type of brain chemical change. These changes cause anxiety, illness and even death. The basic choice is either building more rooms (like the men's group I am involved in or other forms of psychotherapy) or building more cells (to isolate and run from pain). It's one or the other. Reach out to people for support and keep doing it until you get what you want or closing down and seeing nothing but the end.

I love my children. Everything I do now, I do with them in mind. I may have made mistakes as I grew and worked on myself, but I always loved them. Now I soak in the joy that I get when they call me often, see me often and plop the grandkids off with me, so they can have some personal time. I wish I could erase every mistake I made that hurt them or frightened them, but I can't. What I *can* do is proclaim my love for them; it beats with my heart.

For all you readers, I hope you feel this kind of love. I wish you all speed in your own healing and pray that every one of you is able to find strength here. Know that if I can survive the sadistic, physical, emotional and sexual horror of my childhood, then you can survive anything that the world throws at you and break these terrible cycles of dysfunction. Help just one person and make the world a better place for having walked on it.

May you be able to experience the love, hope and connection that I have come to enjoy.

UPDATE: February 27, 2016

Unfortunately, this manuscript has sat idly on my laptop for about three years. After careful thought, I decided to move forward with its intended publication. I had no intentions of watching my father endure any additional stress that would have occurred from the publication of this manuscript; however, I cannot wait any longer. I need to think about all the people this book may help. I have discussed this with my father, and he is now aware of its existence and my intentions. Although I don't believe he is overjoyed by my decision, he nonetheless understands the urgency of this book helping humanity in some little way.

My health has for the most part remained status quo, with the exception of a few more heart attacks and a few more cardiac stents. I am the proud owner of ten, yes, ten cardiac stents. It has changed just how I view the world; some things are less important while others are more. Needless to say, money is not on my list of priorities; other than its ability to buy food, water, shelter and toys, it brings absolutely no value or happiness to a family or relationship. That was a hard lesson for me, as that was the very reason I lived and breathed. What a waste of time and energy!

I am now the proud grandfather of eight beautiful grandchildren and counting. My children and their families are thriving and growing every day. What a thrill to see them grow into fine young men and women without the emotional baggage that I carried. I believe life will be a little less stressful for each of them, and I pray the ripple effect will continue through the future generations. What a beautiful gift for my children, grandchildren and beyond.

I've gone back to school; I am a senior at Temple University majoring in psychology. My destiny has become quite clear; I need to help other victims and survivors of childhood sexual abuse.

And finally, approaching almost thirty-eight years of marriage, I am happy to say my relationship remains strong, no, stronger than it probably ever was. I respect and love Robin very much. I find myself doing little things that I know she likes; when I see the pleasure in her face, I feel really good about myself. We continue to work through the scars that sexual abuse has caused in our sexual relationship. I am still not able to tune out memories of the abuse when Robin and I are intimate. Little triggers are always there that shut me down. I am thinking about trying a different type of therapy called EMDR. This therapy is known as integrative psychotherapy and is used in the treatment of trauma. The results are impressive. Please remember, I am not endorsing this type of therapy, just offering another possible avenue of hope, please research and decide for yourself. Robin has been so patient and understanding. I still believe finding Robin was a product of divine intervention!

Four Generations of Bruckner Men

Mother and Father of the groom dance: Robin and Mike:

Ann Bruckner.
Mike's mom.

David and Ann

Leo and his children
The boys make the paper

DIDN'T NEED 'EM. Royal Navy gun crew aboard Cunard-White Star liner Samaria return 6-inch shells and containers of powder to magazine after arrival here. Samaria had on board 50 children evacuated from Britain and 400 refugees from Nazi-dominated lands.

BOUNCING BABY Mrs. Ann Halbrecht, holding her 14-months-old son, Courtbaugh, arrived on Samaria with strange story. During Nazi raid, bomb smashed through crib where baby was sleeping. Blast tossed baby into air, but she caught him as he fell—unharmed.

SOUVENIRS of Nazi warfare. Alexander Bruckner, 15, and brother David, 11, display pieces of Nazi bombs that fell near their London home.

1940

ETIN—PHILADELPHIA, WEDNESDAY, NOVEMBER 2

Reunion Delayed by Prison Camp

Leo Bruckner, who spent 14 months in German concentration camp, and his family, wide scattered when Nazis annexed Austria, are all together again, at 4833 N. Marshall st. Here Bruckner and his three children: Gertrude, 16; Alexander, 15, and David, 11

LETTER TO MY FATHER – NEVER SENT

Friday, August 4, 1989

Dear Dad,

This letter is the saddest thing I ever had to do. If you cry at any part of it, I guess that's okay because I'm sure I will.

I would like you to know that I miss my father very much and wish he was with me. Someone who could pat my back when I was upset and crying. A dad to hold me when I fell and scraped my knee. And many times a dad who would sit me on his knee and *talk* to me. I know that you didn't have a dad like that either.

Most importantly, I wish my dad would protect me and not let anyone or anything harm me.

I know all this dad stuff must sound awfully corny or stupid to you, but to me, it's vital. Vital to my every breath. Vital enough to keep me alive.

I grieve for your childhood and also grieve for mine because I am *your child*. Let's both pray my children don't grieve for theirs.

Dad, you don't know what you missed. Believe it or not I have a pretty normal life. I'm married and have learned how to spend loving, intimate time with my wife. Imagine that Dad, me, Mike Bruckner learning how to be intimate. Doesn't sound like a priority on either one of our lists.

My children are eight, seven, and three.

Chad is the oldest and going through that eight- to ten-year-old stage. He doesn't like girls (well, just a little) and plays baseball, soccer, and loves to fish and camp and is about to become a Weblo scout. He is a very sensitive, bright child. Chad is entering the fourth grade at Dorothy Simmons School. Dad, I remember when I was in the fourth grade. Do you remember, Dad? He is a very sensitive child who sometimes wears his feelings too close to his sleeve. However, we are both working on that! I love him so much! Now I know what it feels like to have an eldest son.

Lindsay is my little baby girl. I really believe I worship the ground she walks on. The problem is sometimes I don't know much about little girls. Their emotions and feelings are so much different than a little boy's. It kind of rolls off a boy's back, but a girl well, she will remember it for a long time. Because of this, I try to be very careful what I say to Lindsay. Lindsay Leigh Bruckner is probably one of the two most caring people on earth. Lindsay will help anyone at any time. She just loves the feeling of helping. That's her reward. My baby girl is a great student, has a bubbly exhilarant personality, is a daredevil, is at times a little Mommy's girl and at not so often-times a devil worshipper. My heart just starts pumping fast when I see her. She is the love of my life. Lindsay also plays soccer, softball, loves gymnastics and all sports. She is a superfast learner and requires only one look before she can do it. Dad, she's beautiful with long ash blonde hair and big blue eyes with a little button nose set on a freckled face.

On to A.J., our youngest. Wow, he has taught me the meaning of life. He is me. It's just that simple. He feels, I feel. He hurts, I hurt. He laughs, I laugh. You're probably thinking I sound crazy, just read on, and you can stop whenever you feel uncomfortable. Alex John Bruckner is the reincarnated Michael Bruckner. I now know what another three-year-old boy feels, thinks, does, acts, etc., by watching him. They sure act, think, feel *different* than I did. And knowing what the differences are between their childhood and that of myself, it doesn't take long for the pieces to fit. Well enough about that, back to A.J. He is one of my reasons for living. He is handsome (strikingly), bright, energetic, intelligent, cheerful, happy, and most important secure. His security is obvious as he looks at me for reassurance before he steps off the world yet on another mission. Because of these feelings, I watch him *closely*. He sometimes doesn't understand boundaries.

Dad, this may also sound strange to you, but A.J. and I sometimes communicate through looks. We just look at each other, and we know what the other one is thinking and feeling. The other night on vacation, I had a tough time sleeping. In fact, I wasn't sure if I was going to make it through that night, and I went to the bathroom to get a tissue. Well, his bedroom door flew open, and he came running out saying, "Daddy, I'm scared." He has never done that before. Well, anyway, I think you see the point I'm trying to make. If you've ever seen the show *Wonderboy*, then you've seen A.J. He's my little wonderboy.

When I started writing this letter, I didn't know where this letter was taking me to, and it wasn't long after I started that it crystallized.

I'm writing you about my family and hoping you will be able to understand the feelings in this letter.

Robin has been my source of energy for a long time.

A charming, pretty, extremely bright, understanding woman who by the grace of God has remained by my side. It's only recently that I can begin to repay her with such feelings as love, intimacy, respect, and most important, trust! I trust Robin, Dad. She will have had this letter prior to your receipt and shared with me some of the very feelings I had in writing it. Dad, she's a dream come true. Pretty and blonde. (Dad, you hear that I always liked blondes.) The problem is when we're out in public, people stop and stare at her. She is so beautiful. Sometimes, most times, I get a little jealous. But I control myself very well I might add. Robin has played many roles being married to me, that of mentor, villain and victim, and I'm sure not understanding any of them too well. Although we have some similar characteristics from childhood. She now enjoys her new role, that of being my wife and intimate partner. I'm enjoying this as well.

Besides the flaw of being a little right wing (my kids are semi-preppies) and don't worry I won't let her edit this line. Robin is as near to perfection as I can achieve in a wife and partner. She has an exceptionally crisp brilliance about her that lures other people to her. They are quick to learn that Robin is as compassionate and understanding as she is intelligent. This seals the bond for most people as Robin has many relationships, some more intimate than others.

Her loyalty to me has been unshaken, and I love her! Well, you've now had an update on my family. Hope I didn't bore you too much.

From my perspective, it is better and more comfortable for me to write letters. I don't know how you feel or even if you want to communicate at all. I think the communications seem to break down when we see each other. Hope you're taking care of yourself.

Mike

INDEX AND RESOURCES

malesurvivor.org

AllAboutCounseling.com

http://www.allaboutcounseling.com/sexual_abuse.htm

Info on Perpetrators, Statistics, Trauma Recovery, Legal Issues

www.acf.hhs.gov/acf_contact_us.html

www.childhelpusa.org/index.htm

endabuse.org

www.preventchildabuse.com/

www.nlm.nih.gov/medlineplus/childabuse.html#overviews

http://www.childwelfare.gov/

http://www.webmd.com/anxiety-panic/understanding-
    posttraumatic-stress-disorder-basics

ABOUT THE AUTHOR

Mike went back to school at sixty-one to pursue his dreams in the field of clinical psychology. He is a senior at Temple University and hopes to graduate in the spring of 2017 After serving four years in the military, Mike has worked in the insurance industry since 1978. He is the owner of Professional Adjustment Corp, a public adjustment firm that's been in existence since 1998. Mike is married and has eight grandchildren and two more on the way. He lives in the Philadelphia metro area peacefully with his wife, Robin. They have been married for thirty-eight years. His hobbies include football, baseball and saltwater fishing. On weekends, you'll find him puttering in his yard, grooming his fish pond or being a spectator at his grandchildren's many sporting and dance events. After hard, sometimes impossible work, Mike has achieved a level of happiness never before experienced, crediting his wife, children and large extended family for supporting him throughout his journey. Mike has a positive outlook on life. He has survived and thrived.